MILDRED AND ELSIE

The Original Mildred Classics

MILDRED AND ELSIE

Book Three of
The Original Mildred Classics

MARTHA FINLEY

CUMBERLAND HOUSE
NASHVILLE, TENNESSEE

MILDRED AND ELSIE
by Martha Finley

Any unique characteristics of this edition:
Copyright © 2001 by Cumberland House Publishing, Inc.

Published by Cumberland House Publishing, Inc.,
431 Harding Industrial Drive, Nashville, Tennessee 37211.

Cover design by Bruce Gore, Gore Studios, Inc.
Photography by Dean Dixon Photography
Hair and Makeup by Calene Rader
Text design by Julie Pitkin

ISBN: 1-58182-229-4

Printed in the United States of America
1 2 3 4 5 6 7 8 - 05 04 03 02 01

MILDRED AND ELSIE

CHAPTER I

'Tis beautiful when first the dewy light
Breaks on earth! while yet the scented air
Is breathing the cool freshness of the night,
And the bright clouds a tint of crimson bear.

—ELIZABETH M. CHANDLER

A long, long kiss, a kiss of youth and love.

—BYRON

MORNING WAS BREAKING over the landscape. A cool, refreshing breeze, laden with woodland sweets and wild birds' songs, softly kissed Mildred's cheek and awoke her.

She started up with a low exclamation of delight, sprang to the open window, and kneeling there with her elbow on the sill and her cheek in her hand, feasted her eyes upon the beauty of the scene—a grand panorama of wooded hills, falling waters, wild glens and forests and craggy mountains, above whose lofty summits the east was glowing with crimson and gold.

Another moment and the sun burst through the golden gate and began anew his daily round, "rejoicing as a strong man to run a race."

The brightness of his face was too dazzling for Mildred's eyes, and her gaze fell lower down, where wreaths of gray mist hung over the valleys or crept slowly up the mountain sides. Presently it rested on the one of the nearer hilltops, and a sudden, vivid blush suffused her cheek, while a sweet and tender smile shone in her eyes and hovered about her lips.

But a sigh quickly followed, smile and blush faded away, and she dropped her face into her hands with a low-breathed exclamation, "Oh what shall I do? What ought I to do?"

There was a question of grave importance awaiting her decision—a decision which would in all probability affect the happiness of her whole future life on earth. Yea, who should say its influence would not reach even into eternity?

She longed for her mother's counsel, but that mother was far distant and the question one the girl shrank from putting upon paper and trusting to the mails.

But a dearer, wiser, even more loving friend was close at hand, and to Him and His Word she turned for guidance.

Subdued sounds of life came to Mildred's ear as she closed the Book. Servants were astir, setting the house to rights and preparing breakfast for the numerous guests, most of whom still lingered in the land of dreams.

Mildred dressed quickly but neatly, then stole softly from the room, promising herself a stroll through the grounds while the quiet and dewy freshness of early morning yet lingered there.

In one of the wide, cool porches of the hotel, a young man paced to and fro with hasty, agitated step, glancing up again and again with longing impatience at the windows of a certain room on the second floor. Pausing in his walk, he drew out his watch.

"Only a brief half-hour!" he sighed. "Am I not to see her at all?"

But at that instant there stepped from the open doorway a slight, graceful, girlish figure in a dainty white muslin, a bunch of wildflowers in her belt, a broad-brimmed straw hat in her hand. With a low exclamation, "Ah, at last!" he hurried to meet her.

She started slightly at the sight of him and sent a hurried glance this way and that, as if meditating flight.

"Oh, Mildred, don't run away! Why should you avoid me?" he said entreatingly, holding out his hand.

There was a scarcely perceptible hesitation in her manner as she gave him hers.

"Good morning," she said softly. "Is anything wrong? I think you look troubled."

"Yes, I am called away suddenly; must leave within the hour; a dear, only sister lies at the point of death."

His tones grew husky, and her eyes filled with tears.

"Oh, what sad news! I am so sorry for you!" she murmured.

He drew her hand within his arm and led her down a shaded alley.

"It is in your power to give me unspeakable comfort," he said, bending over her. "You wear my flowers;

9

oh, dearest, is not that a whisper of hope for me? You have decided in my favor? Is it not so?"

"Oh, Charlie, don't ask me! I—I have not been able yet to see that—that I may—that I ought—"

"To follow the dictates of your heart? Is that what you would say?" he asked as she broke off abruptly, leaving the sentence unfinished. "Oh, Mildred, you cannot have the heart to refuse me this one crumb of comfort! We must part in a few moments—when to meet again neither of us knows. You have refused to pledge yourself to me, and I will not ask it now— though I solemnly promise you—"

"No, don't," she interrupted, struggling with her tears. "I would have you free, free as air, since I—I can promise nothing."

"I will never marry anyone but you," he said with vehemence. "If I cannot win you, I will live single all my days. But you do care for me? You do love me? Oh, Mildred! One word, only a word or a look, that I may not go away on my sorrowful errand in utter despair. Only assure me that I have won your heart, and I shall never abandon hope that this barrier may some day be removed."

She could not refuse him. She had no power to hide either her love or her grief that they must part, and both had their way for a short space.

He had led her into an arbor whose sheltering vines would screen them from prying eyes. And there, clasped in each other's arms, heart beating against heart, his bearded lip softly touching again and again her cheek, her brow, her quivering lips, they passed the few precious moments that yet remained to them.

Then he was gone, and as the last echo of his departing footsteps died away upon her ear there came over Mildred such a sense of utter desolation as she had never known before. Sinking down upon a rustic bench, she hid her face in her hands and for a few moments allowed her full heart to ease itself in a burst of weeping.

But this would not do! The breakfast hour drew near, and though it had been of late her aunt's custom to take that meal in bed, her uncle would expect to see her in her usual place at the table, and his keen eye would be quick to detect the traces of tears. The cousins, too, would notice them and would not hesitate to inquire the cause.

She hastily dried her eyes, rose, and leaving the arbor, strolled about the grounds, resolutely striving to recover her wonted cheerfulness.

She had made the circuit once, and was again nearing the arbor when she heard her name called in a sweet, childish treble: "Cousin Milly, Cousin Milly!" As she turned in the direction of the sound, little Elsie, closely followed by her faithful mammy, came bounding toward her with a letter in her hand.

"Grandpa said I might bring it to you. Ain't you so glad, cousin?" she asked as the missive was put into Mildred's hand, the sweet baby face held up for a kiss.

Mildred bestowed it very heartily, taking the little one in her arms and repeating the caress again and again, "Very glad, darling," she said, "and very much obliged to my pet for bringing it. Is it time to go in to breakfast, Aunt Chloe?"

"Massa Dinsmore say you will hab time to read de lettah first, Miss Milly," replied the nurse, dropping a curtsey.

"Then I will do so," Mildred said, re-entering the arbor.

"Mat mammy and Elsie stay wis you?" asked the baby girl coaxingly.

"Yes, indeed, darling," Mildred said, making room for the child to sit by her side.

"Dere now, honey, keep quiet and don't 'sturb yo' cousin while she reads de lettah," cautioned Aunt Chloe, lifting her nursling and settling her comfortably on the bench.

Mildred had broken the seal and was already too much absorbed in the news from home to hear or heed what her companions might be saying.

Elsie watched her as she read, with loving, wistful eyes. "Did your mamma write it, cousin?" she asked as Mildred paused to turn the page.

"Yes, dear, and she sends love and kisses to you and wishes I could take you home with me when I go. Oh, if I only could!" said Mildred, bending down to press another kiss on the sweet baby lips.

"Maybe my papa will let me go, if grandpa will write and ask him," returned the child with an eager, joyous look up into Mildred's face. "But I couldn't go wisout mammy."

"Oh, no! if you go, mammy would go, too. You can't be separated from her, and we would all be glad to have her there," Mildred said, softly caressing the shining curls of the little one, glancing kindly up into the face of the nurse, then turning to her letter again.

It was with mingled feelings that she perused it, for though all was well with the dear ones beneath her father's roof, and the thought of soon again looking upon their beloved faces made most welcome the summons home which it brought, there was sorrow and pain in the prospect of soon bidding a long farewell to the darling now seated by her side—the little motherless one over whom her heart yearned so tenderly because of the lack of parental love and care that made the young life seem so sad and forlorn, in spite of all the beauty and wealth with which the fair little one was so abundantly dowered.

As she read the last line, then slowly refolded the letter, tears gathered in her eyes. Elsie saw them and, stealing an arm round her neck, said in her sweet baby tones, "Don't cry, Cousin Milly. What makes you sorry? I loves you ever so much."

"And I you, you precious darling!" cried Mildred, clasping the little form close and kissing the brow again and again. "That is just what almost breaks my heart at the thought of—oh why, why don't you belong to us!" she broke off with a half-stifled sob.

A firm, quick step came up the gravel walk, and Mr. Dinsmore stood looking down upon them.

"Why, what is wrong? Not bad news from home, I hope, Milly?"

"No, uncle, they are all well and everything going smoothly, so far as I can learn from my letter," she said, brushing away her tears and forcing a smile.

"What then?" he asked, "Elsie has not been troubling you, I hope?"

"Oh, no, no, she never does that!"

13

"Breakfast has been announced; shall we go and partake of it?"

"If you please, sir. I am quite ready," Mildred answered as she rose and took his offered arm.

"Bring the child," he said to Chloe. Walking on, he inquired, "What is wrong, Milly? There must have been a cause for the tears you have certainly been shedding."

"I am summoned home, uncle. And glad as I shall be to see it and all the dear ones there again, I can't help feeling sorry to leave you all."

"I hope not. Oh, I wish we could keep you always!" he exclaimed. "But when and how are you to go?"

"Mother wrote that a gentleman friend—our minister, Mr. Lord—will be in Philadelphia in the course of three or four weeks, spend a few days there, then go back to Pleasant Plains, and that he has kindly offered to take charge of me. Mother and father think I should embrace the opportunity, by all means, as it may be a long time before another as good will offer."

"And doubtless they are right, though I wish it had not come so soon."

"So soon?" Mildred returned brightly. "Do you forget that I have been with you for nearly a year?"

"A year is a very short time at my age," he answered with a smile.

But they were at the door of the breakfast room, and the topic was dropped for the present by mutual consent.

CHAPTER II

O my good lord, the world is but a word;
Were it all yours, to give it in a breath,
How quickly were it gone.

— SHAKESPEARE

THE END OF the week found the Dinsmores and Mildred in Philadelphia, very busy with sightseeing and shopping. Each one of the party was to be furnished with a suitable outfit for fall and the coming winter, and Mildred had a long list of commissions for her mother.

Mrs. Dinsmore showed herself keenly interested in the purchase of her own and her children's finery, languidly so in Mildred's. These procured, she immediately declared herself completely worn out and unfit for further exertion.

No one regretted it. Mildred had learned to rely to a great extent upon her own taste and judgment and, with Mr. Dinsmore's efficient help, succeeded quite to her satisfaction in filling out the remainder of her list.

To him fell the task of buying for his little grand-daughter, and Mildred was more than a little gratified by being taken into his counsel and invited to assist him in the choosing of materials and the fashion in which they should be made up.

Despite some drawbacks to her pleasure, mostly caused by Mrs. Dinsmore's temper, Mildred thoroughly enjoyed her stay in the City of Brotherly Love.

It was drawing to a close, when, on coming down from her room one morning and entering the private parlor of their party, she was met by a joyous greeting from little Elsie.

"Oh, Cousin Milly, I'm so glad! Grandpa has got a letter from my papa, and my papa says Elsie must go and buy some pretty presents for all the folks at your house. Isn't that ever so nice?"

"Thank you, darling, you and your papa," Mildred said, stopping to caress the child. "He is very kind, and I know your generous little heart can find no greater pleasure than in giving to others."

"She's a Dinsmore in that," her grandfather said with a proud smile. "They have always deemed it the greatest luxury wealth can purchase. And Elsie is, fortunately, abundantly able to gratify herself in that way, and her father has given her carte blanche (subject to my approval, of course). So, my dear, you are not to object to anything we may take it into our heads to do."

He patted Elsie's curly head as he spoke and looked smilingly into Mildred's eyes.

"You are very kind now and always, uncle," the young girl responded, returning his smile and blushing slightly. "And I don't know that I have a right to object to anything that is not done for myself."

The entrance of Mrs. Dinsmore and her children

simultaneously with the bringing of breakfast put a stop to the conversation.

"Well, Mildred, if it suits your convenience, we will set out at once upon this final shopping expedition," her uncle said as they left the table. Her consent being given, he directed Chloe to make Elsie ready to accompany them.

The child was in her element as they went from one store to another, and she chose, with the assistance of her grandfather and cousin, her gifts to Mildred's parents, brothers, and sisters.

At length, they entered the largest jewelry establishment in the city, and Mr. Dinsmore asked to be shown some of their best gold watches for ladies.

"I am commissioned to select one for a lady friend," he said to Mildred in a grave, half-preoccupied tone as the jeweler promptly complied with his request, "and I want your assistance in making a choice."

"But I am no judge of a watch, uncle," she returned; "Elsie here could select about as well as I."

"Elsie shall have her say about it, too," Mr. Dinsmore said, looking smilingly from one to the other. "All I want from either of you is an opinion in regard to the outside appearance, while this gentleman and I will judge of the quality of the works."

They presently made a selection of both watch and chain satisfactory to all parties. Elsie chose a plain gold ring for Mildred and one for each of her sisters, and they left the store.

Elsie whispered something to her grandfather as he took his seat beside her in the carriage.

He shook his head. "Wait till we get home," he said

rather curtly. "We are going now to choose the new piano."

It was for the drawing room at Roselands, and he took Mildred with him to try the instruments and tell him which she thought the best and finest-toned.

Mildred was equally charmed with several—two in particular—and they had some little difficulty in deciding upon one that should be ordered sent to Roselands.

"I will leave it undecided for today," Mr. Dinsmore said at length, "and will call again tomorrow."

On the way to their hotel and upon their arrival there, little Elsie seemed all eagerness but kept it in check in obedience to an occasional warning look from her grandfather.

Mildred went directly to her room to remove her bonnet and shawl, then sat down in a low chair by the window to rest and think while awaiting the summons to dinner.

She had scarcely done so when there was a gentle tap, as of baby fingers, at her door, and Elsie's sweet voice asked in eager, excited tones for admittance.

"Yes, darling, come in," Mildred answered, and the door flew open and the child ran in, closely followed by her mammy.

The small hands held a jewel case, and the large, soft brown eyes were full of love and delight as she hastened to place it in Mildred's lap, saying, "It's for you, cousin; my papa said in his letter that Elsie might buy it for you." She raised the lid, saying, "See, Cousin Milly, see! Aren't you so glad?"

There lay the watch and chain they had helped Mr. Dinsmore select that morning.

A watch was a far greater luxury in those days than it is now, and this was a costly and beautiful one. Mildred could scarcely believe the evidence of her senses; surely it must be all a dream. She gazed at the child in mute surprise.

Elsie lifted her pretty present with dainty care, threw the chain round Mildred's neck, and slid the watch into the bosom of her dress, then stepped back a little to take a better view. "See, mammy, see!" she cried, clapping her hands and dancing up and down in delight, "doesn't it look pretty on cousin?"

"Jus' lubly, honey. Don't Miss Milly like it?"

Aunt Chloe's look into Mildred's face was half reproachful, half entreating. Could it be possible that her darling's beautiful and costly gift was not appreciated?

"Like it?" cried Milly, catching the child in her arms and covering the little face with kisses, a tear or two mingled with them to the great wonderment of the little one. "Like it? Oh, it is only too lovely and expensive to be bestowed upon me! Sweet pet, you should keep it for yourself. Cousin Milly ought not to take it from you."

"Yes, papa did say so in his letter. Grandpa read the words to Elsie. And when I's big enough, I is to have my mamma's watch."

"But it cost so much," murmured Mildred half to herself as she drew out the watch and gazed at it with admiring eyes.

"My chile hab plenty ob money," responded Aunt Chloe, "and houses and land and eberyting ob dis world's riches. And she lubs you, Miss Milly, and ef

19

you don' take dat watch and chain, she will most break her bressed heart. Won't you, honey?"

The child nodded, and the soft eyes gazing into Mildred's filled with tears. It was impossible to resist their eloquent pleading.

"Then cousin will accept it with her heartiest thanks and will value it more for the sake of the dear little giver than for its usefulness, its beauty, or its cost," Mildred said, holding her in a close, loving embrace. "Dear little girl," she murmured tenderly, "cousin will never intentionally rob you of the smallest pleasure or plant the least thorn in your path."

Another light tap at the door, and Mr. Dinsmore joined them. "Ah! that is right," he said with a smiling glance at the chain about Mildred's neck.

"Uncle, it is too much. I should not have allowed it. How could you?" Mildred asked half reproachfully.

"I only obey orders," was his laughing rejoinder. "Horace feels, as I do also, that we owe a debt of gratitude to your mother—to say nothing of the affection we have for you all. And he knows from the reports I have given him of his child that he could not afford her a greater gratification than the permission to do this. Besides, you have been extremely kind to her and ought not object to her making you some small return in the only way she can."

"Oh, uncle! Her love and sweet caresses have more than recompensed the little I have been able to do for her, the darling!" cried Mildred, heaping fresh caresses upon the little fair one.

Mr. Lord called that afternoon to report himself as arrived in the city and to inquire if it were Mildred's intention to accept his escort on the homeward journey. His stay would be short—just two or three days.

Mildred met him with outstretched hand and eyes shining with pleasure. She had been so long away from home, was so hungry for a sight of anything connected with Pleasant Plains, that had she unexpectedly encountered Damaris Drybread she would probably have greeted her with something like affection.

She perceived no change in Mr. Lord, except that he had a new set of teeth; he seemed to her in all other respects precisely what he was when she bade him goodbye a year ago. But he was astonished, bewildered, and delighted at the change in her. He had always admired her fresh young beauty, but it was as though the sweet bud had blossomed into a half-blown, lovely rose with just a few of its petals still softly folded.

He blushed and stammered, answered her eager inquiries about old friends and all that had been going on in Pleasant Plains since she left in the most absent-minded way, scarcely taking his eyes from her face. In short, he conducted himself as to make his feelings toward her evident to the most careless observer.

"Mildred," said Mrs. Dinsmore, when at last he had taken his departure for that day, "if I were your mother, you should stay from home another year before I would trust you to travel with that man!"

"Why, aunt, you cannot think him anything but a good man!" exclaimed the girl in astonishment.

"Humph! That's a question I don't pretend to decide. But don't, I beg of you, let him persuade you on the way that it is your duty to marry him. If he can only make you believe it's your duty, you'll do it whether you want to or not."

Mildred's cheek flushed hotly. "Oh, Aunt Dinsmore!" she cried, "he could never be so foolish! Why, he's old enough to be my father, and so wise and good, and I am but a silly young thing, as unfit as possible for the duties and responsibilities of a—"

"Minister's wife," suggested Mrs. Dinsmore as the young girl broke off in confusion. "Well, I don't know about that; you are pious enough in all conscience. But, Mildred, you positively must reject him. It would be a terribly hard life, and—"

"Aunt, he has not offered, and I believe, I hope, never will. So I am not called upon to consider the question of acceptance or rejection."

"That was very rude, Miss Keith—your interrupting me in that way," Mrs. Dinsmore said, half in displeasure, half in sport. "Well, if you will allow me, I shall finish what I had to say. I've set my heart on seeing you and Charlie Landreth make a match. There! Why do you color so and turn your head away? Charlie likes you—is in fact deeply in love, I feel perfectly certain, and doubtless will follow you before long. You may take my word for it that he would have proposed before we left the springs if it hadn't been for that sudden summons to his dying sister."

Mildred made no reply. She had kept her face studiously averted and was glad that the entrance, at that moment, of a servant with a letter for Mrs. Dinsmore gave her an opportunity to escape from the room.

CHAPTER III

And 't shall go hard,
But I will delve one yard, below their mines
And blow them at the moon.

— SHAKESPEARE

THE SUN WAS just peeping over the tops of the tall city houses as Mildred entered the carriage that was to convey her to the depot. Mr. Dinsmore and little Elsie — the two whom it was a grief of heart to her to leave — were with her; Mrs. Dinsmore and the others had bidden goodbye before retiring the previous night and were still in bed.

"Elsie, darling, won't you sit in cousin's lap?" Mildred said, holding out her arms to receive the child as her grandfather handed her in at the carriage door.

"No, no! She's much too heavy, and there is an abundance of room," he said hastily.

"But I want to hold her, uncle," returned Mildred, drawing the little one to her knee. "I love dearly to have her in my arms, and this is my last chance."

"As you will, then; a willful woman will have her way," he said lightly, as he settled himself on the opposite seat and the door closed upon them with a bang.

The rattling of the wheels over the cobblestones, as they drove rapidly onward, made conversation next to impossible. But Mildred was not sorry; her heart was almost too full for speech. She clasped little Elsie close, the child nestling lovingly in her arms, while they mingled their caresses and tears.

At the depot, too, where there was a half hour of waiting, they clung together as those who knew not how to part. Elsie's low sobs were pitiful to hear, but she stood in too great awe of her grandfather to indulge in any loud lament.

His kindness to herself had been uniform from the first and continued to the last moment. Not till he had taken her on board the train and made as comfortable as possible did he resign her to the care of Mr. Lord. Then, with a fatherly kiss and an affectionate message to her mother, he left her.

As the train moved slowly on, she caught a last glimpse of him, and of Aunt Chloe standing by his side with the weeping Elsie in her arms.

Mr. Lord essayed the office of comforter.

"That is a sweet child, Miss Mildred, a very sweet child. And Mr. Dinsmore seems a noble man. These partings are sad—especially when we are young—but let the thought of the dear ones to whom you are going, and of the better land where partings are unknown, console and cheer you now."

Mildred could hardly have commanded her voice to reply and was glad the increasing noise of the train relieved her of the necessity for doing so. But she dried her eyes and resolutely forced her tears back to their fountain, calling to mind the lessons on the duty of cheerfulness taught her by her mother, by both precept and example.

And it was joy to know that each mile passed over was bearing her nearer to that loved monitor! What a cheering thought was that! And scarcely less so was the prospect of seeing Aunt Wealthy, with whom she and Mr. Lord were to spend a few days, Lansdale being not far out of their route in crossing Ohio.

In that day there was no continuous line of railroad from Philadelphia to Pittsburgh. They traveled sometimes by stage, passing over the mountains in the latter. This proved the most exciting and perilous part of the journey, the roads being almost all the way very steep and often lying along the edge of a precipice, to plunge over which would be certain, horrible death.

Much of the scenery was grand and beautiful, but the enjoyment of it was greatly interfered with by the sense of danger. Many a time Mildred's heart seemed to leap into her mouth, and she sent up a silent but strong cry to God that He would keep the horses from stumbling, their feet from treading too near the verge.

There was one afternoon so full of terror of this kind—and importunate prayer for preservation— that she felt she could never forget it to the day of her death, even should she live to the age of Methuselah.

The stage was full. The back seat was occupied by our heroine and a young mother with a babe in her arms and another little one by her side; the remaining seats were filled with gentlemen.

"That fellow is drunk and in a terribly bad humor,"

remarked one of the latter as the driver slammed the door to upon them and mounted to his perch.

"In no fit condition to guide those horses over the steep and narrow passes that lie between this and our next halting place," added another uneasily. "You had an altercation with him, hadn't you, Blake?" he said, addressing the first speaker.

"Yes, Mr. Grey, I had. What business had he to hurry us off in this style? Why, we were scarcely seated at the dinner table when he blew his horn—and, and we all had to run to avoid being left."

"Quite true."

"That's so," assented several voices.

"And the same thing is repeated again and again, until it has become quite unbearable," Blake went on, his eyes sparkling with anger. "We pay for our food and have no chance to eat it."

"There seems to be some collusion between the innkeepers and drivers for the purpose of defrauding travelers," remarked Mr. Lord.

"Are we not going very fast?" asked the mother, turning a pale, anxious face toward the last speaker.

"Yes, dangerously so." And, putting his head out the window, he called to the driver, mildly requesting him to slacken his speed.

The reply was a volley of oaths and curses, while the whip was applied to the horses in a way that made them rear and plunge frightfully.

They had been toiling up a steep ascent and now were skirting the mountain side, a high wall of rock on the one hand, a sheer descent of many hundred feet on the other.

Blake glanced from the window with a shudder, turning a ghastly face upon the others. "We shall be hurled into eternity in another minute," he said in a hoarse whisper.

Then voice after voice was raised, calling to the driver in expostulation, warning, entreaty.

"You are risking your own life as well as ours," cried one.

"I tell you I don't care!" he shouted back, with a fearful oath; "we're behind time, and I'll lose my place if I don't make it up. I'll get you to C— by half-past five or land you in Hades, I don't care which."

"Oh, my children, my poor little children!" cried the mother, clasping her babe closer to her breast and bursting into tears. Then, in a sort of desperation, she thrust her head out of the window and shrieked at the man, "For the love of Heaven, driver, have mercy on my poor babes!"

The man was probably a father, for that appeal reached his heart, hardened as it was. There was instantly a very sensible diminution of their fearful velocity, though the stage still rolled on at a dangerously rapid rate, keeping them all in terror until at length it drew up before the door of a tavern where they were to halt for supper.

The gentlemen made haste to alight. Mr. Lord handed out Mildred, then the mother and her children.

"You must be very tired, ladies," he said, following them into the parlor of the inn, which was very plainly furnished with rag carpet, wooden chairs and settee, and green paper window blinds. There was nothing tasteful, nothing inviting, except an appearance of order and cleanliness.

"Yes, sir, I am dreadfully tired," the strange lady answered, dropping into a chair and setting her babe on her knee while she drew the older child to her side and wiped the tears from her cheeks, for she was sobbing pitifully. "That was a fearful ride. The jolting and shaking were bad enough, but the fright was ten times worse. And we're almost starved," she added. "My little Mary is crying with hunger. I hope they'll give us time to eat here. Do you know, sir, how soon the stage starts on again?"

"I will step out and inquire, and also how soon the supper will be ready," Mr. Lord said, moving toward the door.

"Can I do anything for you, Miss Mildred?" he asked, pausing upon the threshold. "You are looking wretchedly pale and fatigued," he added in a tone of concern.

The other gentlemen had gone to the barroom, but at this moment Blake came to a window of the parlor which looked out upon a porch that ran along the whole front of the house. He looked red and angry.

"It seems the same game is to be repeated here," he said, addressing Mr. Lord. "The supper is not ready, and the stage will leave in half an hour. There is every appearance of rain, too. The night will be cloudy and dark, making travel over these mountains doubly dangerous. I propose that we all decide to remain where we are overnight and let the stage go empty. If the whole party will agree in doing so, 'twill serve the rascal right and perhaps teach him a useful and much needed lesson. What do you say, sir? you and your—daughter?"

"My lady friend," stammered Mr. Lord, coloring violently. "What do you think of the plan, Miss Mildred?"

Her cheek, too, flushed a rosy red as she answered eagerly: "Oh, let us stay, by all means! I'm sure it would be better by a great deal than risking our lives on such roads at night."

"Just what I think," said the other lady, "and my little ones are too tired to travel any farther tonight. I shall stay whether the rest do or not. I intend that the children and I shall have a chance to eat one full meal, at any rate," she added to Mildred as the gentlemen walked away together.

The call to supper followed almost immediately upon the announcement that no one would leave in the stage that night.

With the keen appetites they brought to it, our travelers found the fare excellent—good bread and butter, baked potatoes, ham, and fresh-laid eggs.

Mr. Lord, seated between the two ladies, was very kind and attentive to both but as usual did some absurdly absent-minded things.

"Do you really prefer salt to sugar in your coffee, Mr. Lord?" asked Mildred demurely but with a mischievous twinkle in her eye as she saw him draw the salt cellar toward him and dip his teaspoon into it.

She had stayed his hand just in time. "Oh no, certainly not," he said, laughing to cover his confusion as he emptied the spoon into his saucer. "It is a very pleasant evening," he remarked, sugaring his potato.

"Do you think so?" said Mildred, listening to the dash of the rain against the window, for the threatened storm had come. "Then I suppose, like the Shepherd of Salisbury Plains, you are pleased with whatever kind of weather is sent?"

"Certainly we all should be," he said. "But I was not aware till this moment that it was raining."

Mildred, presently becoming interested in some talk going on between her opposite neighbors, had for the moment almost forgotten Mr. Lord's existence. She was recalled to it be a hasty movement on his part. He suddenly pushed back his chair, rose, and walked out of the room.

A glance at his saucer, half full of coffee, then at the laughing eyes of the other lady, enlightened our heroine as to the cause of his sudden exit.

"Salted coffee is not, I found, particularly palatable," he remarked, coming back and resuming his seat. "I am a sadly absent-minded person, Miss Mildred. You should watch over me and prevent such mistakes, as my mother does at home."

"I really do not feel equal to so arduous an undertaking," was her sprightly rejoinder.

"This is a lonely spot, not another house in sight," remarked the mother of the children to Mildred as they returned to the parlor. "I am timid about sleeping alone in a strange place and should like to have a room adjoining yours, if you do not object and are not afraid of being so near a lioness and her cubs," she added with a slight laugh. "I am Mrs. Lyon."

"Mildred gave her name in return and expressed entire acquiescence in the proposed arrangement.

Being much fatigued with their journey they presently retired.

They were up and dressed in time to make sure of their breakfast before the early hour at which the stage was to leave. But they were treated to a repetition of former experiences. The meal was delayed, and they had been scarcely ten minutes at the table when they heard the roll and rumble of the wheels and the loud "Toot, toot!" of the driver's horn as the stage swept round from the stables and drew up before the tavern door.

There was a hasty swallowing down of another mouthful or two; a hurried scramble for hats, bonnets, and parcels; a crowding into the vehicle; and in a moment more it was toiling up the mountain side.

The appetite of no one of the party had been fully satisfied, and there was a good deal of grumbling and complaining from this one and that.

"I tell you, friends," said Blake, "it is high time there was a stop put to this thing. I have an idea in my head, and at the next stopping place, if we are hurried off in the usual style, I want you all to follow my example. If you will, these rascally fellows will find themselves outwitted."

"What is it?"

"What's your plan?" asked one and another, but the only answer was, "Wait and you will see, gentlemen."

"There is one thing I have thought of," Mrs. Lyon said to Mildred, "I'll have my own and the children's bonnets on always before we are called to the meals. If there should be some soiling of ribbons, it will be better than going hungry.

This driver was sober and quiet, the ride, in consequence, less trying than that of the previous afternoon. Between twelve and one they halted for dinner at another country inn.

There was, as usual, a little waiting time, then they sat down to an abundant and very inviting meal but had not half satisfied their appetites when roll of wheels and toot of horn again summoned them to resume their journey.

Every eye in the party turned to Blake. He sprang up instantly, seized a roast chicken by the leg with one hand, his hat in the other, and ran for the stage.

"All right!" cried Grey, picking up a pie. "I'll send the plate home by the driver, landlord," he shouted back, as he, too, darted from the door.

Looking on in dumb astonishment, the landlord saw bread, rolls, butter, pickles, cheese, and hard-boiled eggs disappear in like manner, and before he could utter a remonstrance, the stage was whirling away down the mountain. Not a passenger was left behind, nor nearly so much food as would have remained had they been permitted to finish their meal at the table.

"Outwitted this time, sure as I'm born!" he muttered, at length, turning back into the deserted dining room and ruefully eyeing his despoiled board.

His wife came hurrying in from the kitchen.

"So they're off, and we'll have our dinner now. But," she said, staring aghast at an empty platter, "I say, Jones, where is that chicken? Didn't I tell you that was for ourselves, and you wasn't to put a knife into it?"

"Neither I did," he answered half savagely, "and it's all the worse for us, seein' they've carried it off whole—and if I'd a cut it, there might a been part left on the plate."

"Carried it off!" she cried. "Well, I never! And it was the nicest, fattest, tenderest bit of a spring chicken ever you seen!" With a groan, she began gathering up the empty dishes.

"Take that newspaper out of my coat pocket and spread it over my knees, won't you, Grey?" said Blake, the moment they were seated in the stage. "Now your jackknife, please, and I'll carve this fowl. I fear it'll not be very scientifically dismembered," he said, when his requests had been complied with, "but sufficiently so to enable me to make a tolerably equal distribution. What is your choice, ma'am?" he said, addressing Mrs. Lyon.

The result of their coup d'etat was a very comfortable, enjoyable meal seasoned with many a merry jest over the discomfiture of the foe and the makeshifts they themselves were put to for lack of the usual table appliances.

CHAPTER IV

Alas! my lord, if talking would prevail,
I could suggest much better arguments
Than those regards you throw away on me,
Your valor, honor, wisdom, prais'd by all,
But bid physicians talk our veins to temper
And with an argument new-set a pulse,
Then think, my lord, of reasoning into love.

—YOUNG

BY THE TIME they reached Lansdale, Mildred was weary enough to be very glad of a few days' rest, rest whose delights were doubled and trebled by being taken in the society of her dear old aunt.

The travelers were received with the warmest of welcomes, Mildred embraced over and over again, and Mr. Lord repeatedly and heartily thanked for bringing her.

"Dear child, how you are improved!" Aunt Wealthy said the first moment they found themselves alone together.

"Have I grown, auntie?" Mildred asked with an arch smile, laying two shapely, soft white hands on the old lady's shoulders and gazing lovingly into her

eyes as they stood facing each other on the hearth
rug in front of the open fireplace in Miss Stanhope's
cozy sitting room. It was a cool, rainy evening, and
the warmth of a small wood fire blazing and crack-
ling there was by no means unpleasant.

"Not in height, Milly," Miss Stanhope answered,
giving the young girl a critical survey, "nor stouter,
either. But your form has developed, your carriage is
more assured and graceful, your dress has a certain
style it lacked before, and—but I must not make you
vain," she added, breaking off with her low musical
laugh. "Come tell me all about your Uncle Dinsmore
and his family."

"And little Elsie, the sweet darling!" sighed
Mildred. "Aunt Wealthy she is a perfect little
sprite—the sweetest, most beautiful creature you
ever laid eyes on."

"Ah! I only wish I could lay eyes on her," the old
lady rejoined. "Does she resemble her father in looks?"

"Not in the least. She is said to be the image of her
mother." And from that, Mildred went on to dwell
with minuteness and enthusiasm on all the charms of
the little one, arousing in her companion a very
strong desire to see and know Elsie for herself.

That subject pretty well exhausted, Mildred could
talk of something else, and she found a great deal to
tell about the other Dinsmores, her own experience
in the South, and the incidents of her recent journey.

They had seated themselves on a sofa. Mr. Lord,
suffering from an attack of sick headache, had
retired to his own apartment directly after tea, leaving them to the full enjoyment of each other.

"And have you come back heart whole, Milly, my dear?" asked the old lady, smiling into the eyes of her young relative and softly stroking the hand she held.

The question brought a vivid blush to the fair young face.

"Excuse me, dear child; I do not wish to pry into your secrets," Aunt Wealthy hastened to say.

"No, auntie dear, I do not consider it prying or wish to keep my affairs from your knowledge. You and mother are the two I wish to confide in and consult."

And with many blushes, sighs, and now and then a few quiet tears, Mildred poured out the whole story of Charlie Landreth's and her own love for each other, and the barrier between them, as Aunt Wealthy listened with deep interest and heartfelt sympathy.

"Don't despair, dear child," she said, caressing the narrator in tender, motherly fashion. "Don't give him up. We will join our prayers in his behalf, and the Lord will, in His own good time, fulfill to us His gracious promise to those who agree together to ask a boon of Him."

"Yes, auntie, I do believe He will," Mildred responded, smiling through her tears, "if we pray in faith, for in asking for the conversion of a soul we shall certainly be asking that which is agreeable to His will. And yet—Oh, auntie! it may be long years before our prayers receive the answer, and I—I may never see him again!"

"'Surely goodness and mercy shall follow me all the days of my life,'" repeated Miss Stanhope in low, soft tones. "Milly dear, try to leave the future in the hands of Him who has said, 'I have loved thee with an everlasting love; I will never leave thee, nor forsake thee.'"

Both mused in silence for a little; then Miss Stanhope said, turning with a slight smile toward her young relative, "Milly, child, you are very attractive to the other sex."

Mildred colored and looked down. "Aunt Wealthy," she said, "I hope you do not think me a coquette?"

No, child, no! I'm quite sure you are too kind-hearted to enjoy giving pain to any living creature."

"That is true, auntie; and for that reason I wish none would care for me in that way but the one I can care for in return."

"Yes, and therefore I wish—" Miss Stanhope paused, then in answer to Mildred's inquiring looked concluded her sentence "—that some other escort had been found for you."

Mildred's cheek crimsoned. "Aunt Wealthy!" she exclaimed, "do you—do you really think he cares for me in that way? Oh, I hope not. Aunt Dinsmore said something of the sort, but I hoped she was mistaken."

Miss Stanhope's only answer was a meaning smile and a slight shake of the head.

"Then, Aunt Wealthy, you must help me to avoid being left alone with him!" cried Mildred in a tone of apprehension and annoyance; "and I do hope there will always be other passengers on the boats and stages, so that he will have no chance to say a word."

"I'll do what I can, child. Cling as close to me as you will, but you must rest assured he is bound to speak and have it out with you, sooner or later."

"He shall not if I can prevent him. How can he be so extremely silly! But, indeed, Aunt Wealthy, I think you must be mistaken. He surely has too much sense to fancy me."

"You won't be rude, Milly? You won't forget the respect due to him as your minister?"

"Not if I can help it. Aunt Wealthy, you must help me by not leaving us alone together for a moment!"

"But, my dear, how are my household affairs to be attended to?"

"When we are all together and you want to leave the room, just clear your throat and give me a look, and I'll go first. Then you can readily excuse yourself on the plea of domestic matters calling for your attention, and he may amuse himself with a newspaper or a book until we rejoin him."

Miss Stanhope laughingly agreed to the proposed program, and they carried it out during the whole visit.

Mr. Lord was very desirous to see Mildred alone but found every effort to that end frustrated. Miss Stanhope seemed always in the way, and Mildred would accept no invitation to walk or drive unless her aunt was included in it. He had formerly considered the aunt quite a charming old lady but changed his opinion somewhat at this particular time. Though she was undoubtedly a most excellent woman, and without a superior as a hostess, it was a decided bore to have to listen to and answer her talk when he was longing for a private chat with Mildred."

He bore the trial with what patience he might, comforting himself with the hope of a favorable opportunity for his wooing somewhere on the journey from Lansdale to Pleasant Plains.

Mildred was dreading the same thing and was fully resolved to prevent it, if possible. Therefore, when the stage drew up for them at Miss Stanhope's gate, it was with very different feelings they perceived that it already contained several passengers.

"Safe for the present, auntie," whispered the young girl as they enfolded each other in a last, lingering embrace.

"You can't expect to be so fortunate always," returned the old lady in the same low key and with a humorous look. "Be sure to let me have the whole story in your next letter."

It was staging all the way now. Sometimes they traveled day and night, sometimes stopped for a few hours' rest and sleep at a wayside inn. It was on Monday morning they left Lansdale, and the journey was not completed until Saturday noon.

Through all the earlier part of the route they had plenty of company, the stage being always pretty well filled, if not crowded. Most of their fellow travelers proved intelligent and agreeable—some, both ladies and gentlemen, remarkably so—and the tedium of the way was broken by talk, now grave, now merry, and embracing a wide range of topics.

On one occasion a discussion arose on the propriety and lawfulness of intermarriage between Christians and worldlings. Some took the ground that it was a mere matter of choice; others said that it was both dangerous and sinful for a follower of

Christ to marry any other than a fellow disciple, or one who was esteemed such.

Of these latter, Mr. Lord was one of the strongest and most decided in the expressions of his sentiments and convictions, quoting a number of passages of Scripture to sustain his views.

During the whole of the conversation Mildred was a silent but deeply interested listener, her heart sinking more and more with each word uttered by Mr. Lord; for as her pastor and spiritual instructor, his expressed convictions of truth carried great weight with her and seemed to widen the gulf between herself and him who was the choice of her heart.

Her only comfort was the hope that some day the barrier might be removed. But, ah, many long years might intervene, and who could say that in the meantime Charlie would not grow disheartened and weary of waiting or, incredulous of the love that could keep him waiting, allow some other to usurp her place in his affections?

These were depressing thoughts, and throughout the remainder of the journey they filled Mildred's mind almost constantly. It was only by a determined effort that she could shake them off and talk of other things.

In the course of that day and the next, which was Friday, the other passengers dropped off one by one, until, to her dismay, she found herself alone with Mr. Lord for the first time since they left Lansdale.

The last to leave them was an elderly lady who had been occupying the back seat along with Mildred since the stage had started that morning. When it drew up before her door, Mr. Lord alighted and politely handed her out. On getting in again, instead of resuming his former seat, he took the one she had just vacated.

Mildred's heart gave a throb and the color rushed over her face, for she foresaw what would follow. Still, she would foil him if possible, and perhaps their numbers might be presently again augmented as they rolled onward.

With that last thought in his mind also, the gentleman was disposed to seize his opportunity instantly. He cleared his throat, turned to his companion, and opened his lips, but her back was toward him as she gazed eagerly from the window.

"Look, look at those maples!" she cried. "Was there ever more gorgeous coloring? How perfectly lovely the woods are! And the weather is delightful today. October is the pleasantest month of the year for traveling, I think."

"Any month and any weather would be pleasant to me with you for my companion," he said, "and nothing, my dearest girl, could make me so supremely happy as to secure you as such for the whole journey of life."

She feigned not to have heard or fully understood. "I for one have traveled quite far enough," she responded, still keeping her face toward the window. "I'm tired of it, and of being so long away from the dear home circle. Oh, I am so glad that I shall be with them tomorrow, if all goes well!"

"God grant it, dear Mildred. I shall rejoice in your happiness and theirs, but—"

"Oh see!" she interrupted, pointing to a group of trees near the roadside, "What brilliant reds and yellows! And there! What a beautiful contrast those evergreens make!"

"Yes, God's works are wonderful and His ways past finding out," he answered devoutly, then kept silent, while for some minutes Mildred rattled on, hardly knowing or caring what he was saying so she might but avoid the necessity of listening to and answering the proposal he was evidently so desirous to make.

But his silence disconcerted her. He did not seem to hear her remarks, and at length she found herself too much embarrassed to continue them. For five minutes neither spoke, then he made her a formal offer of his heart and hand, which she gently but decidedly declined, saying she felt totally unfit for the position he would place her in.

He said that in that, he could not agree with her; he had never met any one who seemed to him so eminently fitted for the duties and responsibilities he had asked her to assume. And he loved her as he never had loved and never could love another. Would she not reconsider? Would she not be persuaded?

She told him she highly respected him as a man and a minister, that she felt greatly honored by his preference, but she could not love him in the way he wished.

"Ah," he said, "what a sad blunderer I am! I see I have spoken too soon. Yet give me a little hope, dear girl, and I will wait patiently and do my best to win the place in your heart I so ardently covet."

She could not bring herself to acknowledge that that place was already filled, and he would not resign the hope of finally winning her.

During the rest of that day and the morning of the next, he treated her to frequent, lengthy discourses on the duty of everyone to live the most useful life possible, on the rare opportunities of so doing afforded by the position of minister's wife, and on the permanence and sure increase of connubial love when founded upon mutual respect and esteem, till at length a vague fear crept over her that he might finally succeed in proving to her that it was her duty to resign the hope that at some future day the barrier to her union with the man of her choice would be swept away, and to marry him on account of the sphere of usefulness such a match would open to her.

She heard him for the most part in silence, now and then varied by a slight nod of acquiescence in the sentiments he expressed. Yet even from these scant tokens of favor he ventured to take courage and to hope that her rejection of is suit would not prove final.

It was a great relief to her that they were not alone for the last ten miles that lay between them and Pleasant Plains.

CHAPTER V

Nor need we power or splendor,
Wide hall or lordly dome;
The good, the true, the tender —
These form the wealth of home.

—MRS. HALE

COULD THAT BE home—that pretty, tasteful dwelling, embossed in trees, shrubs, and vines? Mildred was half in doubt, for the house itself seemed to have grown as well as the vegetation that environed it. But yes, the stage was stopping, and there were father and Rupert at the gate, mother and the rest on the porch, every face beaming a joyous welcome.

How Mr. Lord envied them as the stage whirled him rapidly away, out of sight and hearing of the glad greetings!

We will not attempt to describe these but to say that there were close embraces; tears of joy; low-breathed words of tenderness and love, of gratitude to Him who had preserved a beloved child in all her journeyings and brought her to her home again in safety and health; and shouts of delight from the little ones, to whom it seemed half a lifetime since sister Milly went away.

"How we have missed you! Oh, how glad we are to have you back again!" her mother said, looking smilingly at her but with glistening eyes.

"She's changed," said Rupert, regarding her critically. "She's prettier than ever—and something else."

Zillah supplied the words—"more stylish."

"And you! Why, you are a young lady!" exclaimed Mildred, gazing at her in astonishment.

"I'm fifteen and taller than you, I do believe," returned Zillah, laughing and blushing.

"And how you're all grown!" Mildred went on, glancing round the circle.

"Except father and mother," laughed Rupert. "Haven't I nearly caught up to father in height?"

"So you have, and I shall be very proud of my big brother."

"Well, I declare, if you hain't come at last— thought you never was a comin'!" exclaimed a voice behind Mildred. And as she turned quickly about, a toil-hardened hand seized hers in a grasp that almost forced from her a little cry of pain.

"Yes," she said, "I have, and I am very glad to find you here, Celestia Ann. You kept your promise."

"A heap better'n you did yours. Why, you stayed more'n as long agin as you said you was agoin' to when you went off. Had a good time?"

"Yes; but I'm very glad to get home."

"So you'd ought to be. You look downright tired, and I reckon you are all that, and hungry, too. Well, I'll have dinner on the table in about ten minutes." And with the last words, she vanished in the direction of the kitchen.

A look of expectant delight was on every face of the group about Mildred as the mother, saying, "Come, dear child, you will want to get rid of some of the dust of travel," led the way from the room, the others all following.

"Why, the house has grown too," was the young girl's delighted exclamation as she was ushered into an apartment she had never seen before—large, airy, and neatly and tastefully though inexpensively furnished, with white muslin curtains at the windows, a snowy counterpane on the bed, everything new and fresh except the books in the hanging shelves on the wall, and some little ornaments which she recognized as her own peculiar property.

"Yes," her father answered, smiling fondly upon her, "so much so that we shall now have an abundance of room, even with our eldest girl at home. And we hope it will be a very long while before she will want to run away again."

"Yes, indeed, father dear," she said, putting her arms around his neck; "Oh, if you only knew how glad I am to get back!"

"This is your room, Milly; do you like it?" the children were asking in eager tones.

"Yes, yes, indeed! It is perfectly lovely! But, mother, it ought to be yours; it is larger and cheerier than yours."

"Ah! you are assuming to know more than you do, my child," laughed Mrs. Keith. "I, too, have one of the new rooms—there are six in all—and it is in every respect quite equal to this. But make haste with your preparations, for the dinner bell will soon ring."

They lingered at the table, eating slowly, because there was so much talking to be done—such pleasant, cheerful chat.

Then came the opening of Mildred's trunk and the distribution of the purchases she had been commissioned to make, and of her own modest gifts to father, mother, brothers, and sisters, and the more expensive ones from Aunt Wealthy and the Dinsmore relatives. Of these last, little Elsie's were by far the most costly and valuable.

The children were wild with delight, the parents quietly happy in their pleasure, and gratified with the remembrances to themselves.

Mildred exhibited her watch and chain, calling forth exclamations of intense admiration and hearty congratulations.

"Oh, sister Milly, how lovely!" cried Zillah; "I never saw anything so beautiful, and I'm so glad you have it! I don't believe there's another lady in town who has a gold watch."

"No, I presume not," returned Mildred, gazing down upon it with a pleased but rather absent look, "and it is extremely pretty; yet not half so beautiful as the dear little giver." And then she launched into the warmest of eulogies about little Elsie—telling of her loveliness of both person and disposition.

"She must have loads of money to buy you that splendid watch, and all these things for the rest of us," remarked Cyril.

"Yes, indeed! I'd like to be in her place," said Ada.

"I wouldn't," said Mildred, "and I don't believe you would, Ada, if you quite understood her position."

"Why?" the children asked, clustering close about their sister, with looks of surprise and eager interest. "Tell us why. It must be nice to be so rich, to own houses and lands and all sorts of things."

"Do not be too sure of that," said their father. "Though poverty has its trials, wealth brings cares and cannot of itself give happiness. In fact, it has sometimes proved a curse to its possessors. Remember, our Saviour said, 'How hardly shall they that have riches enter into the kingdom of God.'"

"Yes," added Mrs. Keith, "and in another place He says, 'Take heed and beware of covetousness, for a man's life consisteth not in the abundance of the things which he possesseth.'"

"But some rich people are good, aren't they?" queried Cyril. "I'm sure Milly said Elsie was."

"But she's just a baby girl," put in Don, "and maybe she'll get bad by the time she grows up."

"Now, boys, keep quiet, can't you? Let's hear what Milly's going to tell," said Ada.

Mildred glanced at the nearly emptied trunk, the piles of clothing on the bed and chairs, and shook her head. "Another time, children. I ought to be putting these things in place in the wardrobe and bureau."

"Oh, you're too tired! Sit down in the rocking chair and rest while you talk, and I'll help you afterward to arrange your things," Zillah said. With a word of thanks Mildred yielded.

Taking Annis on her lap, and glancing with a smile from one eager, expectant face to another, she asked, "What would any one of you sell all the rest for?"

Several pairs of young eyes opened wide with

astonishment. "Why, Milly, what a question!" "Not for anything!" "Not for all the world! You know we wouldn't!" were the answering exclamations, and then there were loving looks exchanged. Don gave Fan a hug, while Cyril squeezed her hand and patted Annis on her curly head.

"It would be dreadfully lonesome not to have any brothers or sisters!" he said, with a long-drawn sigh of satisfaction.

"Little Elsie has none," said Mildred. "But what if we had no mother, children?"

"Milly, what makes you say such things!" cried Fan, hastily releasing herself from Don and running to her mother to hide her face in her lap with a half-sob.

"No, what's the use?" Zillah asked huskily while Ada's eyes filled and the boys looked distressed, as though the idea was too painful to contemplate.

"Just to convince you that little Elsie is not so much to be envied by us. She has no mother, has never seen her father, and does not know whether he loves her or not."

"Does she show any desire to see him?" asked Mrs. Keith, stroking Fan's hair.

"Oh, yes, mother! Yes, indeed! She talks a great deal about him, often wishes he would come home, and is never more interested than when he is the theme of conversation."

"I hope her grandfather and his wife love her?"

"Not at all; they treat her with almost unvarying coldness and neglect!" Mildred said, her eyes sparkling with indignant anger.

49

Then she went on to tell of various acts of injustice and oppression to which the little girl had been subjected since coming to Roselands, and to give a pathetic description of her loneliness and unsatisfied yearning for the love of her kindred. In conclusion, Mildred asked, "Now would any of you change places with her?"

"No, indeed we wouldn't! Poor dear little thing! We're very sorry for her," the children cried in chorus.

"Mother, mayn't Elsie come here and be your little girl 'long with us?" asked Annis.

"I should gladly take her, darling, if I could," Mrs. Keith answered. "But she belongs to her father, and it is he who directs where she shall live."

"Tell us some more, Milly! Tell about that beautiful Viamede," entreated Ada, putting an arm coaxingly round her sister's neck.

"Some other time, but now I must really go to work and finish my unpacking."

"No, you must go into another room and lie down for an hour or two," said her mother. "You need rest and sleep, and your sisters and I will set things to rights here."

Mildred objected. "Mother, dear, I have come home to ease your burdens, not to add to them."

"And which will you do by wearing yourself out and getting sick?" asked the mother with a merry look and smile. "Set these younger ones a good example by prompt obedience to my direction. We want you bright for a good long talk after tea."

"But, mother, you always have so much to tax your time and strength, and—"

"Run away now, without another word," was the playful reply. "I'm not busy or tired this afternoon."

So Mildred went, slept soundly for a couple of hours, and toward tea time came down to the sitting room, looking quite rested and refreshed, and very sweet and pretty, too, they all thought, in new and tasteful attire and with her glossy brown hair becomingly arranged.

She found her mother and the older girls sewing.

"How nice you look!" Zillah said, surveying her admiringly. "That's a lovely dress and made so prettily! Will you let me have mine made like it?"

"Yes, indeed, and help you make it, too. Mother, how have you managed with the sewing while I've been gone?"

"Pretty well, Milly. Zillah has become quite a needlewoman, and Ada does remarkably well, too, considering her imperfect sight. Housework suits her best on that account. They are dear, helpful girls—both of them."

"Milly, Milly," cried Cyril, rushing in from the grounds, "come and look at our gardens, and our hens and chickens, before it grows too dark."

"The gardens aren't much to look at now," laughed Zillah.

"But she can see pretty well what they have been, and we'll tell her the rest," said Cyril, leading the way.

"Come, girls, we'll all go," Mrs. Keith said, folding up her work. "The rest of the afternoon and evening shall be a holiday in honor of our wanderer's return."

There was, in truth, little to exhibit in the gardens now, save a few late blooming fall flowers, but

Mildred admired them and listened with interest to the accounts given of what had been raised by each little worker during the past spring and summer.

And there was really a large flock of fowl, all in fine condition, promising plenty of eggs and poultry even through the cold winter months, for Rupert had built a snug hen house to protect these feathered friends from the inclemency of the weather.

"Now this way, Mildred. I want to show you the vines I've trained over the front porch," Rupert said.

As they stood looking at the vines, the front gate opened and shut, and a firm, elastic step came quickly up the walk. Mildred turned and found an old acquaintance at her side.

"Wallace — Mr. Ormsby!" she exclaimed, offering her hand in cordial greeting, though the rich color surged over her face with the sudden recollection of his parting words, spoken a year ago.

"No, keep to the first name, please," he said in an undertone, as he grasped her offered hand. "Excuse so early a call, but I did not know how to wait. It seems an age since you went away."

"We are always glad to see you, Wallace," said Mrs. Keith. "You must stay and take tea with us; it is nearly ready. Come, we will all go in now, for the air is growing chilly."

Ormsby was by no means loath to accept the invitation. Mildred seemed to him lovelier than ever, and his eyes were constantly seeking her face when politeness did not require him to look elsewhere. Enchanted anew by her charms of person, manner, and conversation, he lingered for an hour or more after tea, watching, hoping for an opportunity to breathe some words into her ear which should reach no other.

But parents, brothers, and sisters clustered about her, and soon neighbors began to drop in to bid her welcome home — Dr. Grange and his daughter Claudina Chetwood and her brother Will, and one or two others of those who were most intimate with the family. Then a look from Mr. Keith reminding Wallace of an important paper that should be drawn up that evening, he took a reluctant leave.

He paused an instant at the gate to glance back regretfully at the brightly lighted parlor windows and the comfortable-looking group within, of which Mildred was the center.

A tall, muscular figure was approaching from the opposite direction as Ormsby, turning with a sigh, hurried down the street toward Mr. Keith's office. There was an exchange of greetings as the two passed each other. "Good evening, Mr. Ormsby." "How d'ye do, Sheriff?" — and each hastened on his way.

The next moment the tall man was standing where Wallace had been, and now he was gazing intently at the same group, though in truth he scarcely saw any but the central figure — the graceful, girlish form so tastefully attired, the bright, sweet face full of animation and intellect. He could not take his eyes from her — great, dark eyes, hungry and wistful — as for many minutes he stood resting his left hand on the top of the gate, the right arm hanging at his side.

At last, with a sigh that was almost a groan, he, too, turned and went on his way.

"She's prettier than ever—the sweetest thing alive," he murmured half aloud, "and I'll never forgit how good she was to me in that awful time when even my mother couldn't stand by me. But after all that, 'tain't no way likely she cares enough for Gote Lightcap to so much as ask if he's alive or no."

CHAPTER VI

Ah me! For aught that I could ever read,
Could ever hear by tale or history,
The course of true love never did run smooth.

— SHAKESPEARE

THE CALLERS DEPARTED to their own homes. Mr. Keith called the household together and, as usual, closed the day with prayer and praise and the reading of the word of God.

The goodnights were exchanged, and presently Mildred sat alone in her own room, slowly taking down her wealth of rich brown hair while thoughts, half troubled, half pleasurable, were busy in her brain.

A gentle tap on the door, then it was softly opened, and her mother stood by her side.

Instantly the dreamy look left Mildred's eyes, and they were lustrous with love and joy as she lifted them to the sweet face bending over her.

"Darling mother!" she cried, hastening to rise and bring forward the easiest chair in the room, "I'm so glad you have come. I am longing so for one of our old quiet talks."

"Ah! I knew it," Mrs. Keith said, taking the chair. "I saw it in your eyes, dear child, and am as anxious for it as yourself. Oh, it is so nice to have you at home again!"

"And so nice to be here. Mother, dear, there have been times when I felt in sore need of your wise, loving counsel."

Shaking out her abundant tresses, she seated herself on a cushion at her mother's feet and laid her head in her lap, as she had been wont to do in childhood days.

"Then I trust you carried your perplexities to a wiser Friend, whose love is even greater than that of the tenderest mother," Mrs. Keith said, gently caressing the silken hair and the blooming cheek.

"Yes, mother. Ah! what could I have done without that Friend?"

Then, with blushes and tears, she pored out the story of her love and of her refusal to engage herself because the chosen of her heart was not a Christian.

Mrs. Keith was a little surprised, a trifle disappointed. "I had almost set my heart on having Wallace for my future son-in-law," she remarked in a playful tone, "and no such objection could be brought against him."

"No," said Mildred, half averting her blushing face; "he is good and noble and true—a sincere Christian, I do believe, and I heartily respect and like him. But, oh mother, why is it that the course of true love never will run smooth?"

"I think it does sometimes, at least often enough to prove the rule."

"I was in hopes it might have been out of sight, out of mind with Wallace," Mildred said presently.

"No, Cupid's arrow had gone too deep for that. But perhaps it may prove so with the other, and you may yet learn to care for poor Wallace."

"No, mother, I am quite sure that I can never give him anything but the sisterly affection that is already his. Mother, I know girls who think it must be a delightful thing to have number of lovers, but I don't find it so. There is so much that is painful and perplexing connected with it."

"Perplexing, my child?"

"Yes, mother. Do you—do you think it can ever be the duty of one who cannot marry the man of her choice to become the wife of another because it will open to her a wider sphere of usefulness?"

"Why that question, Mildred?" asked Mrs. Keith in grave surprise.

"Because Mr.—Mr. Lord thinks I ought—that it is my duty to—to marry him; and though he did not convince me, he—he made me afraid it might be."

A mirthful look had come into Mrs. Keith's eyes.

"My dear, silly little girl," she said, bending down to get a better view of the blushing face, "why did you not tell him you are quite unfit for the position he offered you?"

"I did, mother," Mildred answered with sincere humility, "but he—still insisted. He has somehow formed a very mistaken opinion of me."

"That is a pity; but we will not let him sacrifice himself. I shall refuse consent, and so will your father."

"But don't you think him a good man?" Mildred asked, lifting her head and gazing into her mother's eyes with a look of mingled relief and perplexity.

"Very good, but very unsuitable in disposition and in years for a husband for you, or a son-in-law for me. His absent-mindedness would put a great deal of care on your young shoulders. But, my dear, leaving the question of his character and suitableness in other respects entirely out of sight, the fact that you prefer another is quite sufficient in itself to make your acceptance of his suit both foolish and wrong.

"Nothing can make it right for man or woman to marry one while his or her heart turns more strongly to another. As to his argument that thus a wider sphere of usefulness would be opened to you, all I have to say is that it is not—cannot ever be—right to do evil so that good may come."

Mildred drew a long sigh of relief. "Oh, mother, I am so thankful that you take that view of it! And I am sure it is the right one. You have lifted half my load, but—"

"Can you not cast the other half on the Lord?"

"I do try to. But, mother, what do you think? Would it be wrong for me to—"

"Follow the dictates of your heart?" Mrs. Keith asked as Mildred paused, leaving the sentence unfinished. "My child, that is a question for you to settle with your own conscience. You have God's holy word to guide you, and in answer to prayer He will give you the guidance of the Spirit also. I will only say that it cannot be other than a dangerous experiment for a Christian to enter into the closest of earthly relations with one who is living for this world alone."

"Especially one so weak and ready to wander out of the way as I," sighed the young girl.

"Well, darling, you are young enough to wait, and let us hope all will come right at length. Ah, we may be sure of it, for 'we know that all things work together for good to them that love God, to them who are the called according to His purpose.' But it is growing late, and you ought to be resting after your long journey." And with a tender goodnight they parted.

Mr. Lord filled his own pulpit the next day, both morning and evening, preaching with acceptance to his flock.

Mildred attended both services but carefully avoided meeting the speaker's eye during the sermon, and slipped out of the church as quickly as possible after the benediction was pronounced. Each time she was delayed a little in her exit by the necessity of stopping for a shaking of hands and the exchange of a few words with friends and neighbors who stepped forward to greet and welcome her home. But others were crowding about the minister with the same kindly intent, and thus unconsciously assisted in her desired avoidance of him.

She was little less anxious to escape Wallace Ormsby, but in that she was not so successful. He walked by her side in the morning as far as their roads lay in the same direction, yet as Don held fast to one of Mildred's hands and Fan to the other, his talk was only on topics of general interest, the sermon, the Sunday school, etc.

In the evening, as she stepped into the vestibule, she saw Wallace waiting near the outer door, and read his purpose in his eyes. She turned to Zillah, who was close beside her, seized her hand, and, holding it fast, whispered in her ear, "We'll walk home together. Be sure to keep close to me."

Zillah nodded with a roguish smile and, to Wallace's great annoyance, did as requested. Offering one arm to Mildred, he could do no less than ask Zillah to take the other, which she did with alacrity. And all the way home she kept up a constant stream of talk, Mildred listening with inward amusement, Wallace wondering whether it was with a purpose and wishing she was somewhere out of earshot of what he wanted to say to her sister.

The Keiths neither paid nor received visits on the Sabbath, so he bade the girls good evening at their father's door and quietly wended his way to his lonely bachelor quarters over the office. The girls, listening to his departing footsteps, exchanged a few words of congratulation on the one side and thanks on the other, mingled with a little girlish laughter at his expense.

"Mother," said Mildred, as they were preparing for bed, "I will be up in good season tomorrow morning and get breakfast, as Celestia Ann will of course be busy with her washing."

"You'll do no such thing," cried Zillah. "Ada and I will get breakfast and dinner tomorrow, and you're not to so much as put your nose into the kitchen. You're to play lady for a week at least while you look on and see how nicely we can manage without you."

"I've played lady long enough, and—"

"Mother, isn't it to be as I've said?" demanded Zillah, not giving Mildred time to finish her sentence.

"Yes, Milly, you and I can find enough to do out of the kitchen for the present, and we will let these young cooks have a chance to show what they can do," Mrs. Keith said, looking from one to the other with a proud, fond, motherly smile.

"I like to cook," put in Ada. "Milly, I can make nice cakes and desserts; they all say so. And Zillah and I made pickles and preserves this fall, mother only overseeing and telling us how. Celestia Ann wanted to turn us out of the kitchen and do it all herself, but mother said no—we must learn how."

Monday morning found the Keith household like a hive of cheerful, busy bees. Mrs. Keith and Mildred, busy together in the dining room, washing and putting away the breakfast china and silver, which were never allowed to go into the kitchen, laid plans for the fall and winter sewing.

"I have learned to cut and fit, mother," Mildred said, "taking lessons from one of Aunt Dinsmore's servants who is excellent at it. So now, if you like, I shall fit all the dresses of the family, beginning today with Ada's and Zillah's calicoes."

"I'm very glad, my dear," Mrs. Keith replied, "for really there is not a competent dressmaker in town. But I see I shall have to take care that you do not over-work yourself," she added with an affectionate smile.

"Mother," said Zillah, putting her head in at the door, "we're nearly out of salt and sugar both. Who shall go for them?"

"Cyril and Don. It is a lovely day, and they will enjoy the walk. Mildred, there will be some little articles wanted for our dressmaking; suppose you go also and select them. The walk will be good for you, and you will like to see how the town has grown in your absence."

Fan and Annis put in an eager plea to be permitted to be part of the party.

Mildred demurred. "I'm afraid, Annis, darling, you can't walk fast enough. Sister Milly wants to come back quickly because of the sewing."

"Never mind that. We will not deprive the darling of so great a pleasure merely to save a few minutes," the mother said, turning a loving smile toward the little, disappointed face, which instantly grew bright again. "Linger a little on the way, Mildred, and enjoy the sweet air and the beauty of the woods. These things were given for our enjoyment."

"Dearest mother! Always so kind and thoughtful for each one of us," Mildred whispered, bending over her mother's chair to kiss the still fresh and blooming cheek.

Mildred had returned to her home entirely restored to health, full of the old energy, and with a desire to accomplish a great deal in the way of relieving her mother's cares and burdens and promoting material interests of each member of the family of loved ones. She had planned to do a certain amount of the sewing that day and was eager to begin, but she was learning the difficult lesson of readiness to cheerfully yield her own plans and wishes to those of others, remembering that "even Christ pleased not Himself."

With a face as bright and sweet as the lovely October morning, she made herself ready and set out on her errand, Fan clinging to one hand, Annis to the other. The two little boys now brought up the rear, now hastened on in front or trotted alongside, as inclination dictated.

"Yonder comes the sheriff; we'll meet him in a minute," said Cyril presently.

"Who is sheriff now?" asked Mildred.

"Gotobed Lightcap. He's learned to write with his left hand, and they 'lected him sheriff last week. Everybody voted for him because they were so sorry for him. Wasn't it nice? Mother says the folks in this town are the kindest people in the world, she thinks."

"Yes, it was nice and kind," Mildred responded, looking a little curiously at the tall, broad-shoul-dered, masculine figure approaching from the oppo-site direction. In dress, in gait, in the intelligence of his countenance, he was an improvement upon the Gotobed of two years ago.

In another moment they had met. He lifted his hat with his left hand and bowed a little awkwardly, while a deep-red flush suffused his swarthy face.

Mildred colored slightly, too, but greeted him cor-dially and without any show of embarrassment, inquiring after his health and that of his family.

We're all as well as common, thank ye, Miss Keith," he said, devouring her face with his eyes. "And I hope you're the same and as glad to git back as all your friends is to see ye."

"Thank you, I do find it nice to be at home again," she responded, bowing and passing on.

Their way lay past her father's office. Ormsby, looking up from the deed he was drawing and catching a glimpse of her graceful figure as she hurried by, sprang up and stepped to the door just in time to see her go into Chetwood and Mocker's.

He was on watch for her as she came out again and waylaid her with an invitation to drive out with him that afternoon.

"Thank you," she said with a winsome smile, "I fully appreciate your kindness, but—don't you think, after my long vacation, I ought now to stay at home and work? I had planned to do a good deal of sewing today."

"But the weather is so fine, and we ought to take advantage of these lovely days, which will so soon be gone," he said persuasively. "Let the sewing wait; 'twill be just the thing for the stormy days that will soon be upon us. "Yes," she answered, laughing and nodding goodbye.

Zillah met her at the door, her eyes dancing with fun. "Mr. Lord's in the parlor with mother, and you're wanted there, too."

"Oh, dear!" sighed Mildred, but throwing off her hat in the hall, she went at once to meet the ordeal.

The gentleman rose on her entrance and with beaming eyes and outstretched hand came eagerly forward to greet her. "My dear Miss Mildred, I have been telling your mother of my plans and wishes, and asking her consent and approval of my—the proposal I made to you the other day, and—"

"And she has declined to give them?" Mildred said, allowing him to take her hand for an instant, then hastily withdrawing it, her eyes seeking her mother's face while her own flushed crimson.

"Yes, I have been trying for the last half hour to convince Mr. Lord how entirely unsuitable you are for the place and position he offers you," Mrs. Keith answered in a grave, quiet tone. "Come and sit down here by me," she said, making room for her on the sofa by her side, "and we will try together to convince him."

"That will be no easy task," remarked the middle-aged lover as Mildred hastened to accept her mother's invitation. Then, standing before them and fixing his eyes admiringly upon the blushing, downcast face of the maiden, he went on to plead his cause with all the force and eloquence of which he was master.

He spoke very rapidly, as if fearful of interruption and determined to forestall all objections, Mildred listening in some embarrassment and with much inward disgust and impatience.

These changed directly to almost overpowering mirthfulness, as the man, perhaps finding his false teeth, to which he was not yet fully accustomed, impeding his speech to some extent, in his intense interest in his subject and hardly conscious of the act, jerked them out, and twirled them about in his fingers for an instant. Then, with a sudden recollection, he thrust them in again, his face turning scarlet with mortification and the last word faltering on his tongue.

Controlling her inclination to laugh, Mildred seized her opportunity. "Mr. Lord," she said with gentle firmness, "please do not waste any more words on this subject, for I have no other answer to give you today than that which I gave before. Nor shall I ever have any other. I highly respect and esteem you, feel myself greatly honored by your preference, but—it is utterly out of my power to feel toward you as a woman should toward the man with whom she links her destiny for life."

With the last word she rose and would have left the room, but he intercepted her. "Not now, I suppose. Ah, my foolish impatience, which has a second time betrayed me! But I will wait—wait years, if—"

"It is useless, quite useless, I assure you," she interrupted in some impatience. "To convince you of that, I will acknowledge that—that my heart has already been given to another."

Hiding her blushing face in her hands, she hurried from the room, leaving to her mother the task of consoling the rejected suitor.

Mrs. Keith afterward reported that he stood for a moment as if struck dumb with surprise and dismay; then muttering, "Wallace Ormsby—it must be he," was rushing bareheaded from the house when she called him back and gave him his hat and a consolatory word or two, which he did not seem to hear, as he merely turned about without replying and walked rapidly away with the hat in his hand.

Mildred, hurrying to the privacy of her own room with cheeks aflame and an indignant light in her brown eyes, found herself intercepted by Zillah.

"Good girl not to say yes," cried the latter merrily, putting her arm round Mildred's neck and kissing her.

"What do you mean, Zillah? You don't know anything about it," Mildred said repulsing her slightly and averting her face.

"Yes, I do. Mr. Lord's been asking you to marry him—I knew by his looks that that was what he came for—and I'm glad you won't have him. He's nice enough as a minister, but he's too old and ugly and awkward for a husband for my pretty sister Milly. Wallace Ormsby would be far more suitable, in my humble opinion," she added with a merry twinkle in her deep blue eyes.

Mildred looked at her and took a sudden resolution. "Come in here," she said, pushing open her room door. "Zillah, can you keep a secret?"

"Suppose you try me," was the laughing rejoinder.

"I will. I am sure I may trust you."

So Zillah presently knew how matters stood between her sister and Charlie Landreth, and Mildred felt that she had another hearty sympathizer and was safe from any more teasing about Wallace Ormsby from that quarter.

As for the latter, he of course improved his chance as they drove together that afternoon over the prairies and through the beautiful autumn woods—and Mildred had the painful task of crushing his hopes as she had already crushed those of her older admirer.

❧ ❧

CHAPTER VII

A mighty pain to love it is,
And 'tis a pain that pain to miss;
But of all pains, the greatest pain
It is to love, but love in vain

— COWLEY

"OH, WALLACE, FORGIVE me! Not for worlds would I have hurt you so if—if I could have helped it." Mildred's voice was full of tears, and she ended with a sigh that was half a sob.

His head was turned away so that she could not catch so much as a glimpse of his face.

"It is just what I expected when you went away," he answered huskily; "but I don't blame you. I've always known I wasn't half good enough for such a girl as you."

"No, don't say that!" she cried, almost eagerly. "You are good enough for anybody, Wallace. You are noble and true and brave, and father says that with your talent and industry you are sure to make your mark in the world."

"What do I care for that now?" he returned bitterly. "You have been my inspiration, Mildred. It was for you—to win you and to make you rich and happy—that I have studied and toiled and planned, and now you are lost to me!" he groaned.

"Oh, Wallace!" she murmured softly, "I had hoped yours was a higher ambition—that you had consecrated your time, talents, everything, to Him who gave them and whose love is better beyond comparison than any or all earthly loves."

"You are right," he said after a moment's silence, and his voice was low and humble. "It ought to be so; it shall be so henceforward. But—oh, Mildred, what happiness can there be in life without you!"

I will be your sister, Wallace; I have a real sisterly affection for you."

"I ought to be thankful for even that—I shall be someday. But oh, Mildred! Now it seems like giving me a crumb when I am starving, so famished that nothing less than a whole loaf will relieve the dreadful pain. And this other fellow that has won you away from me—will he—will he take you away from us soon?"

"No, Wallace, not soon, perhaps never," she answered in low, quivering tones.

He turned and faced her with an inquiring look. "I have misunderstood. I thought you said the—affection—was mutual."

"I will tell you all about it," she said after a moment's embarrassed silence. "I think I owe you the confidence as some slight amends for the pain I have unwillingly caused you."

Then, in a few words, she told him just how matter stood between Charlie Landreth and herself, withholding only the name of her favored suitor.

When she had finished, silence fell between them for many minutes. Mildred's eyes were cast down, Wallace's gazing straight before him or taking note of the inequalities of the road. They were nearing the town when at last he spoke again.

"I thank you for your confidence, dear Mildred — you will let me call you that this once? You know I shall never abuse it. I am sorry for your sake that he is not all you could wish, but don't let it make you unhappy. I couldn't bear that. And I hope and believe it will all come right in the end."

"Wallace, how good and noble you are!" she cried, looking at him with eyes brimming with tears. "We will always be friends — good, true friends, shall we not?" she asked almost beseechingly, holding out her hand.

He caught it in his and pressed it to his lips with a low, passionate cry. "Oh, Mildred! Can I never be more than that to you?"

An hour later Mrs. Keith found her eldest daughter in her own room, crying bitterly.

"My dear child! what is the matter?" she asked in concern.

"Oh, mother, mother, I seem to have been born to make others unhappy!" sobbed Mildred.

"I have often thought you were born to be the great comfort and blessing of your mother's life, and I have thanked God with my whole heart for His good gift to me," the mother said with a loving caress. And a glad smile broke like sunlight through the rain of tears.

"Mother, what a blessed comforter you are!" sighed Mildred, resting her wet cheek on her mother's shoulder. "Mother, Wallace loves me and seems almost brokenhearted because I—I cannot return it. And he is such a dear, noble fellow, too—worthy of a far better wife than I would make!"

"We must try to convince him of that and make him glad of his fortunate escape," Mrs. Keith said in her playful tone.

Mildred laughed in spite of herself, but a little hysterically. Then, growing grave again, she said, "But, mother, he does really seem heartbroken, and it is dreadful to me to have caused such suffering to one so deserving of happiness."

"I do not doubt it, my dear, and I feel for you both, but trouble does not spring out of the ground. All our trials are sent us for some good purpose by the best and dearest of all friends, who knows just what each one of us needs and never makes a mistake. I am sorry for you both, but I do not think either is to blame, and I believe you will come out of the trial better and happier Christians than you would ever have been without it.

"Now, dear child, I shall leave you, so that you may be able to spend a few minutes with that best Friend before joining us downstairs. Try to cast all your care on Him, because He bids you do so and because it is for your happiness."

Mildred followed the kind, wise advice and then, having done what she could to remove the traces of her tears, hastened to join the family at the tea table in answer to the bell.

Her mother adroitly contrived to take the attention of the others from her, and no one noticed that she had been weeping.

The faces and the chat were cheerful and bright, as was almost invariably the case in that family circle, and the joy of being among them again after so long an absence soon restored Mildred to her wonted serenity.

They discussed their plans for study and work for the coming fall and winter months. The town was still destitute of a competent teacher; therefore, Mildred proposed to resume her duties as governess to her younger brothers and sisters. She could assist Rupert, too, in some areas and wished to perfect herself in some and to improve her mind by a course of reading.

Then, as always, there was the family sewing and various housekeeping cares of which she desired to relieve her mother.

Zillah listened with a mirthful look to Mildred's long list and at its conclusion asked, with a merry laugh, "Is that all, Milly?"

Mildred echoed the laugh and blushingly acknowledged that it was very much easier to plan than to execute, and she feared she should fall very far short of accomplishing all she desired.

"Yes," said her father, "but it is best to aim high, for we are pretty sure never to do more than we lay out for ourselves, or even so much."

"But if Milly undertakes all the work, what are Ada and I to do?" queried Zillah, in a sprightly tone.

"She'll be glad enough before long to let us help with it," remarked Ada quietly. "If she'd had breakfast and dinner to get today, she couldn't have walked out this morning. And I don't think she could have taken time to drive out this afternoon if she had been the only one to help mother with the sewing."

"No, that is quite true," said Mildred, smiling at Ada's serious face, "and I'm delighted to find what helpful girls you two have become, for there is an abundance of work for us all."

"Enough to leave us no excuse for idleness," added the mother, "but not so much that any of us need feel overburdened, for 'many hands make light work.'"

"Especially when the head manager knows how to bring system to her aid," concluded Mr. Keith with an affectionate, appreciative glance at his wife.

"Yes," she rejoined brightly, "very little can be accomplished without that. But with it I think we shall do nicely."

The little ones were asking when lessons were to begin.

"Tomorrow, if mother approves," answered Mildred.

Her father smiled approval, remarking, "Promptness is one of Mildred's virtues, one we may all cultivate with profit."

"I quite agree with you, Stuart," Mrs. Keith said, "and yet it is sometimes best to make haste slowly. Mildred, my child, you have had a long, wearisome journey and may lawfully rest for at least this one week."

"And we all need our new clothes made up," remarked Ada. "Mother, have Milly make your black silk dress first."

Mildred and Zillah chimed in at once, "Oh, yes! Certainly mother's dress must be the very first thing to be attended to."

"I can fit it tonight," said Mildred.

"And I cut off the skirt and run the breadths together," added Zillah.

"Come, come, you are entirely too fast," laughed Mrs. Keith. "I will not have any one of you trying her eyes with sewing on black at night. We will all work this evening on the calicoes begun today, and Milly shall fit a calico for me before she tries her hand on the silk. But we will give this week to sewing and reading. Cyril can read nicely now, and he and Rupert shall take turns reading aloud to us. Lessons shall begin next Monday."

Aside from her desire to be as helpful as possible to her dear ones, Mildred felt that constant employment for head and hands was the best earthly antidote for her present griefs and anxieties. So she plunged into study and work, and gave herself little time for thought about anything else, and her mother, understanding her motive, not only did not oppose but encouraged her in that course.

Some new books she had brought in her trunk proved a rare treat to the entire family, and work, enlivened now by the reading of these and now by cheerful chat, was decidedly enjoyable.

There were many calls, too, from old friends and acquaintances, and so the week slipped away very quickly and pleasantly.

Saturday's mail brought Mildred a letter from Charlie Landreth, which gave her both pain and pleasure.

The ardent love to her that breathed in every line sent a thrill of joy to her heart, yet it bled for him in his deep grief for the loss of his sister, grief unassuaged by the consolations of God.

Her prayers for him went up with increased fervor. Earnestly, importunately, she besought the Lord to comfort him in his great sorrow and to make it the means of leading him to a saving knowledge of Christ Jesus.

Then she sat down and answered his letter with one that, through all its maidenly modesty and reserve, breathed a tender sympathy that was like balm to his wounds and a cordial to his fainting spirit when at length it reached him.

Mildred desired to have no secrets from her wise and dearly loved mother. Both Charlie's letter and her own were carried to her, and the latter was submitted to her approval before it went on its mission of consolation.

This communication from him whose love found a response in her own heart did good service in banishing from her mind, in great measure, disturbing thoughts about the other two suitors.

For some weeks they absented themselves from the house, then gradually resumed their former intimacy with the family. Mildred met them, when compelled by circumstances, without embarrassment, but she avoided a meeting when she could without seeming to do so purposely.

Chapter VIII

A delightful surprise

"There is a letter, my dear, which concerns you quite as much as myself," Mr. Keith said, putting it into his wife's hand. "It gives information which perhaps for several reasons, it may be as well for us to keep to ourselves for the present," he added with a smile. "That is why I kept it back until now that we are alone."

They had retired to their own room for the night, and the little ones who shared it with them were fast asleep.

"From Uncle Dinsmore!" Mrs. Keith exclaimed, recognizing the handwriting at a glance.

Her husband watched her face with interest and some curiosity as she read, a slight smile on his lips and in his eyes.

She looked up presently with hers shining. "How wonderfully good and kind they always are!"

"Almost too kind," he responded, his face clouding a little. "At least I wish there was no occasion for receiving such favors. I should have been tempted to decline, had I been consulted beforehand. But it would hardly do now that the goods are almost here. We could not well send them back."

"No, certainly that is not to be thought of for a moment," she said, lifting her face to his, eyes smiling through tears. "We must follow the Golden Rule, Stuart, and accept their kind assistance in educating our children, just as we would wish them to accept ours were our situations reversed."

"Yes," he said, heaving a sigh, "doubtless you take the right view of it. But—ah! Marcia, wife, 'it is more blessed to give than to receive.'"

"It is indeed, my dear husband, and we will not refuse them that blessedness now but will receive their kindnesses in the spirit in which they are offered, hoping that we may have our turn some of these days. Shall we not?"

He gave a silent assent. "Do you not agree with me that it will be well to keep the matter a secret from the children until the boxes arrive?" he asked.

"Oh, yes, indeed! We will not let even Mildred know. It will such a delightful surprise to her, dear child, for though she has uttered no word of complaint, I am sure it must have been a great disappointment to her that you could not furnish her with a piano this fall to enable her to keep up her music. Now she can do that and teach her sisters, too."

"And her playing will be a great treat to us all," added Mr. Keith with a smile that spoke volumes of fatherly affection and pride in his firstborn.

"And the books! What delightful times we shall have over them!" she added, eyes sparkling. "What a help they will be in cultivating our children's minds! I think our dear girl must have completely won her way into the hearts of my uncle and cousin Horace."

"As her mother did before her," he responded with a light, happy laugh.

When preparing to leave Ohio for the wilds of Indiana, Mr. Keith had sold most of the family's heavy articles of furniture, among them the piano. Its loss had been greatly lamented, especially by the older girls and Rupert. The purchase of another had become a darling project with him, and to that end he had worked and saved till he had now quite a little hoard, earned mostly by the sale of fruits, vegetables, and fowl of his own raising, his mother paying him for these at the market price and whatever surplus he had finding ready sale at the stores.

The lad was very industrious and painstaking, generally very successful in what he undertook — as such people are apt to be — and while generous to others, spent little on himself.

Since Mildred's return, the desire for a piano was stronger than ever. There was not one in the town, nor an organ, nor any kind of keyed instrument, so that there was no chance for them to hear her play and judge of her improvement. And worse still, she would be in danger, from want of practice, of losing all she had gained. But pianos cost a great deal in those days, and Mr. Keith could not just spare the money to make the purchase and pay the heavy cost of transportation.

Money was scarce in that region then, and business was conducted very largely by barter. This made it easier for him to accommodate the expense of enlarging his house than to pay for something that must come from a distance.

There was little or no fretting or complaint over this state of things, but the children often talked longingly of the good time coming, when father would be able, with the help of what they could earn and save, to send for a piano.

That time seemed to be brought a little nearer by an act of thoughtful kindness on the part of their dear Aunt Wealthy. She had set apart from her income a certain sum that she engaged to send to their mother, at regular intervals, to be divided among them as pocket money. The dear old lady could hardly have devised anything that would have given more pleasure. The news, as announced by Mildred on the day of her arrival, was received with demonstrations of wild delight, and evidently the little ones now considered themselves moneyed individuals, taking great pride and pleasure in consulting together, or with father and mother, as to the disposal of their incomes.

This opened up to the careful Christian parents a new opportunity for the study of the natural character of each of their children and the curbing of wrong inclinations, whether toward extravagance or stinginess.

One day, several weeks after Mildred's return, Rupert came in near the dinner hour and, drawing his mother aside, whispered something in her ear. There was a look of covert delight on his face, and his eyes sparkled as he added, "One's long, low and broad, mother; can only be one thing, I think—just the thing we're all wanting so much. But where could it come from?"

"Where do you suppose?" she answered merrily.

"Well, the instant you are done your dinner you may go down and see them brought up."

"But father said it was your wish and his to make it a complete surprise to the children."

"Mildred included?" laughed his mother; "You are so much older than she. I will manage it. They shall be out of the way while we unpack."

Mr. Keith came in presently, and with his arrival came the call to dinner.

Mildred looked curiously at Rupert several times during the meal, wondering at his unaccustomed air of importance, the half-exultant, meaning glance he now and then sent across the table to one or another of their parents, and the haste with which he swallowed his food and hurried from the table and the house, having asked to be excused, for he had business of importance to attend to.

"Dear me, what airs!" laughed Zillah as he whisked out of the room. "One would think he was a man, sure enough."

"Girls," said Mrs. Keith, "I want you to take the little ones out for a walk this afternoon. It is a bright day and the walking good, and if you are all well wrapped up, you will not feel the cold."

"Not if they go at once," put in Mr. Keith.

"Run away and make yourselves ready, all of you."

"The party will be large enough without me, won't it, mother?" queried Mildred. "You know I have a piece of sewing on hand that I am very desirous to finish before night."

"Let it go, child. You need air and exercise far more that I do the dress," was the smiling rejoinder.

Then came a chorus of entreaties from all the children that mother should go too.

But she would not hear of it, having a matter of importance to attend to at home. Perhaps, if tomorrow should prove pleasant, she would go with them then.

And so with smiles and loving words she helped to make them ready and sent them on their way.

She was barely in time, for hardly were they out of sight when a wagon drove up with two large, weighty-looking boxes. Rupert and two men, besides the driver, were in the vehicle also, and it took all their strength, with Mr. Keith added, to lift and carry the boxes into the house.

"Oh, it is a piano! I know it is!" cried Rupert as they set down in the hall the box he had described to his mother.

"A pianer did ye say?" queried one of the men, as for a moment they all stood panting from their exertions and gazing down upon the burden they had just deposited upon the floor. "Let's get it open quick then, for I never see one in my life."

Rupert ran for the hatchet, and in another five minutes the lid was off the box and all remaining doubt vanished.

"It is, it is!" cried the lad, fairly capering about the room in his delight. "Oh, what a joyful surprise for the girls and all of us! But where on earth did it come from? Father—"

"I had nothing to do with it, my son," Mr. Keith asserted with a grave earnestness that precluded the idea that he might be jesting.

The boy looked bewildered, then disappointed. "There's been some mistake, I'm afraid. Perhaps there's another family of our name somewhere in this region, and —"

But his mother whispered a word into his ear, and his face grew radiant. "Is that it? Oh, mother how good they are!"

"Let's git the thing out and see what it's like," said the man who had spoken before.

The others eagerly assented and set to work at once, Mr. Keith giving assistance and directions, Mrs. Keith pointing out the place in the parlor where she wished it to stand.

"You kin play, I s'pose, Mrs. Keith. Won't you give us a tune?" was the eager request when their task was ended.

Smilingly she seated herself and played *Yankee Doodle* with variations.

They were delighted. "First rate!" commented the one who seemed to act as chief spokesman for the party. "Now, ma'am, if you please, won't you strike up *Hail Columby*?"

She good-naturedly complied, added *The Star Spangled Banner*, then rose from the instrument.

They thanked her warmly, saying they felt well paid for bringing "the thing" in.

"You must come in again someday, if you enjoy hearing it," she said with gracious sweetness. "I think you will find my daughter a better performer than I am."

"Yours is plenty good enough for me," they answered, bowing themselves out.

"It is a very sweet-toned instrument," she remarked, running her fingers over the keys, "a most magnificent present. How delighted Mildred and the rest will be!"

"I am eager to witness it," her husband said with a smile. "It is indeed a most valuable gift, and nothing could have been more acceptable."

"They're the kindest, most generous relations anybody ever had," added Rupert emphatically. "What's in that other box? Shan't we open it now?"

"Books," answered his mother. "Yes, we may as well open it and spread them out ready for Mildred's inspection. Most of them belong to her."

This done, Mrs. Keith again seated herself at the piano.

The young people had taken a long walk, moving briskly to keep themselves warm, for the November air was frosty. They were now returning in merry spirits, eyes sparkling and cheeks glowing with health and happiness, while the tongues of the little ones ran fast and a joyous shout or a silvery laugh rang out now and then, for the greater part of their way lay not through the streets of the town, but on the outskirts — along the river bank, through the groves of saplings, and over still unoccupied prairie land. When they came where there were houses and people to be disturbed by their noise, their mirth subsided a little, and they spoke to each other in subdued tones.

As they drew near home, unaccustomed, surprising sounds greeted their astonished ears.

"Oh, what's that music?" cried the little ones. "Such pretty music!"

"Why, it sounds like a piano!" exclaimed the older ones, "but where could it come from?" They rushed tumultuously into the house, even Mildred forgetting the staid propriety of her years.

The parlor door stood open, and—yes, there it was!—a beautiful piano, mother's skillful fingers bringing out its sweetest tones, father and Rupert standing enraptured close beside her, and Celestia Ann, sleeves rolled up, dish towel in hand, eyes dancing, and mouth stretched in a broad grin, stationed at the farther end.

"Well, I never! Where on airth did the critter come from?" she exclaimed just as the others came upon the scene. "I never seen the like, I never did!" she went on. "I just ran down town of an arrant, and I'd come home again and in the back door and begun to wash up them dishes when I heered this agoin', and come in to find out what under the sun was agoin' on."

But no one seemed to hear a word she said; the children were jumping and careering about the room in frantic delight, clapping their hands, pouring out questions and exclamations. "Oh, aren't you glad? Aren't you glad?" "Isn't it a beauty?" "It's just too nice for anything!" "Who did send it?"

Mildred stood silently gazing at it, her eyes full of glad tears. Father and Rupert were watching her, taking no notice of the others.

"Well, dear?" her mother said, whirling about on the piano stool and looking up into her face with tender, loving eyes.

"Oh, mother, it is too much!" she cried, the tears beginning to fall. "Uncle Dinsmore sent it, I know, and I do believe it's one of the very two I liked the best of all we saw. He bought the other for themselves and this for us."

"For you, dear. But indeed it is, he says, not his own gift, but Cousin Horace's. The books are from him—our kind, generous uncle." And she pointed to them where they lay, piled high upon the table.

"Books, too!" Mildred exclaimed in increased astonishment and delight.

"Yes, he has marked out a course of reading for you—subject to your father's and my approval—and sent the necessary books and some others besides."

While his wife was speaking, Mr. Keith had drawn near and put an arm about Mildred's waist, and now she fairly broke down. Hiding her face on her father's shoulder, she sobbed aloud.

The children were immediately awed into silence. They gathered around her, asking in half-frightened tones, "Milly, Milly, what's the matter? Are you sorry the piano's come? We thought you'd be so glad."

"And so I am," she said, lifting her head and smiling through her tears.

Her mother vacated the stool, her father seated her thereon, and hastily wiping away her tears, she sent her fingers flying over the keys in a lively, merry tune that set the children to jumping and dancing more wildly than before.

Chapter IX

Labor in the path of duty,
Gleam'd up like a thing of beauty.

— Cranch

"My dear child, you have improved wonderfully," Mrs. Keith said as Mildred concluded a much longer and more difficult piece of music than the one with which she had begun.

"She has indeed! I'm quite proud of her performance," echoed Mr. Keith.

"She does make terrible fine music," put in Celestia Ann; "but I wisht she'd stop a bit, or them dishes o' mine'll never git washed."

"And I must go to the office," said Mr. Keith, looking at his watch and glancing about in search of his hat.

"And I to my sewing," added Mildred, rising.

The children entreated somewhat clamorously for more but yielded their wish at once on mother's decision that they must wait till after tea.

"Oh, the books!" cried Mildred, springing toward them with an eager gesture. "But no," she said, turning away with a half sigh, "I must not take time to even look at them now."

"Yes, you may," her mother said smilingly. "Glance at the titles and dip in here and there, just to whet your appetite. Read this note from your uncle, too, and then we can talk over your plans for mental culture while we're busy with our needles."

"Always the same kind, indulgent mother," Mildred said with a look of grateful love. "I will do so, then, and try to work fast enough afterwards to make up for lost time."

Half an hour later she joined her mother and sisters, who were all sewing industriously.

"Such a nice note, mother. Shall I read it to you?"

"Yes, if you like. I always enjoy uncle's letters."

"It sounds just like his talk," Mildred said when she had done reading, "saying the kindest things half jestingly, half earnestly. But the idea of his thinking I must have wondered that he gave me no special parting gift—when he was all the time heaping favors upon me!"

"But it was Cousin Horace who gave the piano," said Ada.

"Yes, and uncle the books. Now I must strive to show my appreciation of their kindness by making the best possible use of both presents."

"For your own improvement and that of others," added her mother. "I want you to lend them, one at a time, to Effie Prescott and poor Gotobed Lightcap."

"What about him, mother?" Mildred asked, taking up her sewing. "The children told me he had been elected sheriff."

"Yes. I was very glad. He deserves every encouragement, for he is trying to educate himself, and I really hope some day may be able to enter one of the learned professions."

"Poor fellow!" Mildred exclaimed feelingly, tears starting to her eyes as memory brought vividly before her the sad scene connected with the loss of his right hand. "He is welcome to the use of any or all of my books. I will gladly do anything in my power to help him."

"Now, suppose we talk about ourselves and our own affairs," Zillah suggested in her sprightly way. "I'm extremely anxious to learn to play on that lovely piano but don't see how either you, mother, or Milly is to find time to give me lessons, for you are both busy as bees now from morning to night."

"And I want to learn, too," put in Ada imploringly.

"So you shall, dears, both of you, if you continue to be the good, industrious, helpful girls you have been for the past year," the mother said, displaying her cheery smile. "Milly and I will manage it between us. Almost all our winter clothes are made now, so that we will not need to give so much time to sewing as we have for the past month or more."

Mildred seemed to be thinking. "I believe we can manage it," she said presently. "I hear the recitations from nine to eleven now, you know. We must begin at eight after this, and then from ten to twelve can be spared for the two music lessons."

"And afternoons and evenings you must reserve for yourself—your exercise, study, reading, and recreation," added Mrs. Keith, "while I oversee the practicing and the preparation of lessons for the next day. Two music lessons a week to each will be all-sufficient. Yes, I am sure that with system and rigid economy of time—making good use of each golden minute as it flies—we can accomplish all that is necessary, if not all that is desirable."

Again a few moments of thoughtful silence on Mildred's part, then she said, "Mother, do you think I ought to take that Sunday school class? I don't feel fit, and—and besides, it will take a good deal of my time to attend right to it—prepare the lessons and occasionally visit the children through the week."

"I would have you consider the question carefully and prayerfully and in the light of God's holy word, which is our only rule of faith and practice, daughter. 'As we have therefore opportunity, let us do good unto all men.' 'He that winneth souls is wise.'"

"But, mother, I am not wise."

Mildred's tone was low and humble.

"'If any of you lack wisdom, let him ask of God, that giveth to all men liberally, and upbraideth not; and it shall be given him.' Ask for it and search the Scriptures for it, for we are told, 'The entrance of Thy word giveth light; it giveth understanding to the simple.' And while you study it for the benefit of others, you will be cultivating your own soul—a matter of even greater importance than the culture of your intellect."

"And I could not do the first without at the same time doing the last."

"No; that is very true. Also, I trust, daughter, that your great motive for improving your mental powers is that you may thus be prepared to do better service to the Master?"

"I hope so, mother; it is, if I know my own heart," Mildred said, looking up with shining eyes. "I know it is said that duties never conflict, yet it does seem sometimes as though they did."

"As for example?" Her mother's eyes smiled encouragingly and sympathizingly into hers.

"Why, there is the weekly church prayer meeting to take one whole evening out of the six."

"Only from an hour to an hour and a half," corrected Mrs. Keith.

"But it breaks into the evening so that one can hardly do much with the leavings," Mildred said with a slight laugh. "And then the young girls' prayer meeting breaks up one afternoon of every week, and besides—oh, mother! It is a real trial to me to lead in prayer, and I am sure to be called on."

"I hope you will never refuse," Mrs. Keith said gently and with a tender, loving look. "We should never fear to attempt any duty, looking to God for help, for it shall be given, and a blessing with it."

"It is a great cross to me."

"Greater than that the Master bore for you?"

"Oh, no, no! Nothing to compare to it, or even to what many a martyr and many a missionary has done and borne for Him."

"And is it not a blessed privilege to be permitted to do and bear something for His dear sake?" Mrs. Keith asked in tones trembling with emotion.

"Oh, mother, yes!" And Mildred's head bowed low, a tear falling on her work.

"Oh, my darling, be a wholehearted Christian!" the mother went on, speaking with intense earnestness. "Consecrate yourself and all you have to the Master's service—time, talents, influence, money—everything you possess. He gave himself for us; shall we hold back anything from Him?"

"Oh no! But mother—"

"Well, dear?"

"Shall I not do better service by and by, perhaps, by now giving my whole time, energy, and thought to preparation for it?"

"Do you find that you can always do a given amount of mental work in a given space of time?"

"No, mother, sometimes my brain is so active that I can do more in an hour than I can sometimes accomplish in a day."

"And cannot He who made you and gave you all your mental powers cause them at any time to be thus active? My child, He never lets us lose by working for Him; in some way He will more than make it good to us. 'He that watereth shall be watered himself.' 'Seek ye first the kingdom of God, and His righteousness; and all these things shall be added unto you.'"

Mildred looked up brightly. "I think—I am sure you are right, mother, and I will take up all those duties, trusting to the dear Master to help me with them and with my studies. My time is His, as well as all else that I have."

"Yes, 'ye are not your own, for ye are bought with a price; therefore glorify God in your body and in your spirit, which are God's.'"

"Who, mother?" asked little Fan, playing with her doll nearby.

"All God's children, my child."

"I want to be one, mother. But who bought them? And what with? What price?"

"Christ bought them with His own precious blood."

"Mother," said Ada softly, "how good He was! I wish I could do something for Him, but I'm not old enough to teach in Sunday school or pray in the prayer meeting."

"No, darling, but you can pray at home, kneeling alone in your own room, and join with your heart in the prayers at family worship and at church. You can pray in your heart at any time and in any place for yourself and for others. In His great kindness and condescension God listens to our prayers at all times, if they come from the heart, and just as readily to those of a little child as to those of the wisest and mightiest of men."

"Oh, mother, I'm glad of that! But if I could do some work for Him I'd love to do it."

"Do you remember, dear, that once when Jesus was on earth the people asked Him, 'What shall we do that we might work the works of God?' and Jesus answered and said unto them, 'This is the work of God, that ye believe on Him whom He hath sent.'"

"That was Jesus Himself," the child said thoughtfully, staying her needle in midair while her eyes sought the floor. "Mother, could you tell me just what is meant by believing on Him so as to be saved? It can't mean only believing all the Bible says about Him is true, because it tells us 'the devils also believe, and tremble.' I heard father read it from the Bible at worship this morning."

"Yes, my dear child, it does mean much more than that," the mother said as she silently asked the help of God to make it clear to the apprehension of all present, even to little Annis, who leaned confidingly against her knee, the blue eyes gazing earnestly into her face.

"The devils know the truth, but they don't love it," she said. "God's children do; they are glad that He reigns and rules in all the universe. But the devils gnash their teeth with rage that it is so and would tear Him from His throne if they could."

The two little boys were in the room, Cyril whittling, Don poring over a new book that Mildred had brought him from Philadelphia. The one shut his jackknife, the other his book, and both drew near to listen.

"Jesus didn't die for them, did He, mother?" asked Cyril.

"No, my son, there is no salvation offered them. And God might justly have left us in the same awful condition, but of His great love and mercy He has provided a wonderful way by which we can be saved. 'For God so loved the world that He gave His only begotten Son, that whosoever believeth in Him should not perish but have everlasting life.'

"Faith is another word that means the same as believing. The Bible tells us that without faith, it is impossible to please God; also, that the faith which availeth anything worketh by love. 'Unto you, therefore, which believe, He (Jesus) is precious.' The faith that please God and will save from sin and eternal death loves the Lord Jesus Christ and trusts for salvation only in what He has done and suffered for us."

"We can't do anything to save ourselves, mother?"

"We cannot do anything to earn our salvation; we can have it only as God's free, undeserved gift. We have all broken God's holy law, but Jesus kept it perfectly in our stead. Our sins deserve God's wrath and curse, both in this life and that which is to come, for it is written, 'Cursed is every one who continueth not in all things which are written in the book of the law to do them.' But Jesus has borne that curse for all His people. 'Christ hath redeemed us from the curse of the law, being made a curse for us.'"

"I should like to have that right kind of faith if I knew just how to get it, mother," said Ada.

"'By grace are ye saved, through faith; and that not of yourselves, it is the gift of God,'" quoted Mrs. Keith. "Ask for it, my child. Jesus said, 'Every one that asketh, receiveth'; and again, 'If ye shall ask anything in my name I will do it.'"

"You know, my child, that though we cannot see Him, He is always near. Go to Him in prayer, confess your sins. Tell Him that you are altogether sinful by nature and by practice, and can do nothing at all to deserve His favor, but that you come in His name, pleading what He has done and suffered for you, because He has invited you so to come. Ask Him to take away your wicked heart and give you a new one full of love for Him. Accept His offered salvation from sin and hell. Give yourself to Him, and He will take you for His own, for He says, 'Him that cometh to me I will in no wise cast out.' He will give you true faith and true repentance — sorrow for sin because it is displeasing to God, a sorrow that will lead you to hate and forsake it, and to be a follower of God as a dear child, doing Him service from the heart, striving to please, honor, and glorify Him in all things, not that you may be saved but because you *are* saved."

"But what can a little girl like me do for Him, mother?"

"Or a boy like me or Cyril?" added Don.

"Christ is our example, and one thing the Bible tells us of Him is that when He was a child on earth, He was subject to his parents; that is, he obeyed and honored them. You must do the same by yours, if you would be His disciples.

"There are few, comparatively, whom God calls to do what men consider great things for Him. But if we do faithfully each little everyday duty—it may be only to learn a lesson, to sweep or dust a room, to make a bed, go on an errand, or something else quite as simple and easy—because we want to please and honor Him, he will accept it as work done for Him. Men can judge only from appearances; God sees the heart, the motives, and whether they are good or bad determines whether He is pleased or displeased with our acts."

"Mother," cried Ada, looking up with a glad smile, "how nice that is! Any work must be sweet when we think of God watching and being pleased with us for doing it just as well as we can because we love Him."

"Yes, daughter, love is a great sweetener of labor of whatever kind it may be."

CHAPTER X

True faith and reason are the soul's two eyes,
Faith evermore looks upward and descries
Objects remote.

—QUARLES

MR. KEITH AND Wallace Ormsby were busy, each at his own desk. Unbroken silence had reigned in the office for the last half-hour, when suddenly dropping his pen and wheeling about in his chair, the elder gentleman addressed the younger:

"Why, how's this, Wallace? I haven't seen you in my house or heard of your being there for weeks. What's wrong?"

Wallace, taken by surprise, could only stammer out rather incoherently something about having had a good deal to do—"correspondence and other writing, studying up that case; you know, sir."

"Come, come, now, you're not so hard pushed with work that you can't take a little recreation now and then," returned his interrogator kindly. "And I really don't think you can find a much better place for that than my house; especially since Mildred's at home again."

"That is very true, sir," said Wallace, "but—I'd be extremely sorry to wear out my welcome," he added with a laugh that seemed a trifle forced.

"No fear of that, Wallace, not the slightest," Mr. Keith answered heartily. "Why, we consider you quite one of the family; we can never forget how kindly you nursed us in that sickly season. And we've a new attraction."

"Yes, sir, so I heard. A very fine instrument, isn't it?"

"Yes; if we are judges. Come up this evening and hear Mildred play. I think she has really a genius for music, but that may be a fond father's partiality."

The invitation was too tempting to be declined. It had taken a very strong effort of will to enable the lovesick swain to stay so long away from his heart's idol, and now under her father's hospitable urgency, his resolution gave way.

"Thank you, sir; I shall be delighted to come. I have no doubt Miss Mildred is quite as fine a performer as you think her," he said as each resumed his pen.

Mrs. Keith, with strong faith in the wisdom of the old adage "All work and no play makes Jack a dull boy," always insisted upon each member of her household taking a due amount of recreation. The older girls would sometimes, in their eagerness to finish a piece of work or learn a lesson for the morrow, be ready to take up a book or sewing immediately on leaving the tea table, but their mother put a veto upon that, and by precept and example encouraged a half-hour of social chat, romping with the little ones, or gathering about the piano to listen to

Mildred's playing. And often, a little time before tea was given to music, both vocal and instrumental, with everyone, even down to little Annis, frequently taking part in the latter.

This season of mirth and merriment was over for the evening, and Mrs. Keith had taken the younger children away to put them to bed. Zillah and Ada were at their tasks in the sitting room, but Mildred still lingered at the piano, feeling that she had need of practice to recover lost ground.

Mr. Keith listened for a little longer and then, remarking that he must see Squire Chetwood about a business matter, donned his hat and overcoat and went out.

Rupert stood beside his sister, turning the pages of her music and praising her execution. "I'd like all the town to hear you," he said.

"I should prefer a much smaller audience," she returned laughingly. "Ru, did you remember to mail that letter?"

"No, I didn't!" he cried, in some consternation.

She drew out her pretty watch.

"There's time yet," he said, glancing at its face, "so I'm off."

Hurrying out of the front door, he encountered Ormsby in the front porch.

"Hello! Is that you, Wallace?" he cried. "A little more and there'd have been a collision. Haven't seen you here for an age! Been wondering what had become of you. Well, walk right in. You'll find Milly in the parlor. But you must excuse me for awhile as I've a letter to mail."

He held the door open as he spoke, and having seen the caller inside, hastily shut it without waiting for a reply to his remarks and rushed away.

The parlor door stood ajar. Wallace tapped lightly, but Mildred, intent upon her music, did not hear, and he stole quietly in. He stood for a moment almost entranced by the low, sweet tones of voice and instrument.

Mildred was thinking of Charlie, and her voice was full of pathos as she sang:

> *"When we two parted*
> *In silence and tears,*
> *Half broken-hearted,*
> *To sever for years."*

A deep sigh startled her, and she turned hastily to find—not Charlie but Wallace regarding her with eyes full of despairing love mingled with tender compassion.

He saw that her eyes were full of tears, and coming quickly to her side, he took her hand in his.

"Dear Mildred, I can't bear to see you unhappy," he said, in low, tremulous tones. "Don't grieve, it will come right someday. Ah, if only I could have won your heart!" And again he sighed deeply.

"It's the old story, 'the course of true love never will run smooth,' and we can only be sorry for each other," she returned with forced gaiety, hastily wiping away her tears. "Take a seat, won't you, and I'll give you something more cheerful than that sickly sentimental stuff you caught me singing. That is, of course, if you wish to hear it." She looked up into his face with an arch smile.

A tete-a-tete with him at that time was not desirable—would be rather embarrassing. She wanted to avoid it and heartily wished some one of the family would come in immediately. Thus, she was not seriously displeased at the sudden and unexpected entrance of Celestia Ann.

This very independent maid-of-all-work came bustling in, dressed in her "Sunday best" and with a bit of sewing in her hand.

"Good evenin', Mr. Ormsby," she said, nodding to him. Then, turning to Mildred, she added, "I declare, Miss Mildred, your playin' is so powerful fine I couldn't noways stand it to set out there in the kitchen while the pianer was agoin' in here and nobody to listen to it. You see, I thought you were alone, but I reckon Mr. Ormsby won't mind me."

Wallace was too well aware of the value of the woman's services and the difficulty of retaining them to make any objection. He merely nodded and smiled in reply to her salutation. Then, turning to Mildred, he answered her with, "Indeed, I should be delighted. In fact, your father invited me to call this evening for the express purpose of listening to your music, and," he added in a whisper, "though I feared my visit might not be altogether welcome to you, I had not the courage to deny myself so great a pleasure."

"There was no occasion," Mildred said, in the same low tone. "We all want you to feel yourself quite at home here. You'll excuse the intrusion of—"

"Oh, certainly; I understand it."

Celestia Ann had seated herself beside a lamp burning on a distant table and was industriously plying her needle.

"Come, give us a lively tune, Miss Milly, won't ye?" she said. "*Yankee Doodle* or *Hail Columby* or some o' them tunes folks dances to."

"Which or what will you have, Mr. Ormsby?" asked Mildred.

"I?" he said with a smile; "Oh, I own to sharing Miss Hunsinger's partiality for our national airs and am well satisfied with the selections already made."

Mildred gave them in succession.

A tall man with a book under his arm stood in a listening attitude at the gate. Mrs. Keith, seeing him from an upper window, came down and opened the front door.

"Good evening, Mr. Lightcap," she said in her pleasant voice, "won't you come in out of the cold?"

"I come to fetch back your book, Mrs. Keith," he said, moving toward her with long strides, "and I thought I'd not disturb the folks in your parlor by knockin' whilst that music was agoin'. I'm a thousand times obleeged fer the loan o' the book, ma'am;" she said and he handed it to her, then lifted his cap as if in adieu.

"No, no, don't go yet," she said. "I have another book for you, and you must have some more of the music, if you care to hear it, without standing in the cold to listen.

Her pleasant cordiality put him at his ease, and he followed her into the parlor.

Mildred was playing and singing *The Star Spangled Banner*, Wallace accompanying her with his voice, both so taken up with the business at hand that they did not perceive the entrance of Mrs. Keith and Gotobed until they joined in on the chorus. Mildred looked up in surprise and nodded a smiling welcome to the latter.

"I tell you, that's grand!" he exclaimed at the close, his face lighting up with patriotic enthusiasm. "There's somethin' mighty inspirin' about them national airs o' ourn. Don't ye think so, Mrs. Keith?"

"Yes," she said, "they always stir my blood with love for my dear native land, and awaken emotions of gratitude to God and those gallant forefathers who fought and bled to secure her liberties."

"Ah!" he sighed with a downward glance at his mutilated arm, "I can never lift sword or gun for her if occasion should come again!"

"But you may do as much, or even more, in other ways," she responded cheerily.

"I can't see how, ma'am," he returned with a rueful shake of the head.

"'Knowledge is power.' Intellect can often accomplish more than brute force. Go on cultivating your mind and storing up information, and opportunities for usefulness will be given you in due time," she answered with her bright, sweet smile. She turned with a cordial greeting to Lu Grange and Claudina and Will Chetwood, who were being ushered in at that moment by Celestia Ann, who now took her departure to the kitchen—probably thinking Miss Mildred had listeners enough to be able to spare her.

The piano was a new and powerful attraction to the good people of Pleasant Plains, and all the friends and acquaintances of the Keiths—as well as some whose title to either appellation was doubtful—flocked to hear it in such numbers that for two or three weeks after its arrival Mildred seemed to be holding a levee almost every evening.

"How my time is being wasted!" she sighed one evening as the door closed upon the last departing guest.

"No, dear, I think not," responded her mother with an affectionate look and a kindly reassuring smile. "You are recovering lost ground—perfecting yourself in facility of execution and giving a great deal of pleasure, and it is no small privilege to be permitted to do that last—to cheer heavy hearts, to lift burdens, to make life even a little brighter to some of our fellow creatures. Is not that so?"

"Yes, mother, it is, and yet I find it very trying to have my plans so often interfered with."

"Ah, my child, we must not allow ourselves to become too much attached to our plans," returned Mrs. Keith with a slightly humorous look and tone, and passing her hand caressingly over Mildred's hair, "for all through life we shall be very frequently compelled by circumstances to set them aside."

"Is there any use in making plans, then?" the girl asked half impatiently.

"Surely there is. If we would accomplish anything worthwhile, we must lay our plans carefully, thoughtfully, wisely, and then carry them out with all energy and perseverance. Yet we must not allow ourselves to be impatient and unhappy when providentially called upon to set them aside. 'It is not in man that walketh to direct his steps,' and we ought to be not only willing to bend to God's providence but glad to have Him choose for us."

"Yes, mother—yes indeed!" Mildred murmured, a dewy light coming into her eyes. "If one could only always realize that He sends or permits these little trials, they wouldn't be hard to bear, for it is sweet to have Him choose for us."

It so happened that this was the last of that trial of Mildred's patience. A storm set in that night which lasted for several days, keeping almost everybody at home. Then came weeks of ice and snow, making fine sleighing, skating and sliding, and thus furnishing other and more exciting amusement to the residents of the town, both old and young.

The Keiths took their share in these winter pastimes—Mildred as well as the rest, often doing so to please her mother rather than herself yet always finding enjoyment in them.

'Twas a busy life she had led that winter and by no means an unhappy one, in spite of the obstinate refusal of the course of true love to run smooth.

It came to a rougher place, to deeper, swifter rapids, in the ensuing spring.

Through all these months of separation she and Charlie had kept up a correspondence, though at somewhat irregular and infrequent intervals. A much longer time than usual had now passed, and her last letter to him still remained unanswered. She was secretly very much disturbed in mind, sorely troubled lest some evil had befallen him, though not permitting herself to doubt for a moment that his love for her remained as strong and fervent as ever.

At last a letter came. Rupert brought it from the office at noon and handed it to her with a meaningful smile and a twinkle of fun in his eyes.

"Something to brighten this dull, rainy day for you, sis," he said merrily.

"Thank you," she returned, flushing rosy red, and her heart giving a joyous bound as she slipped the missive into her pocket.

"What? You're not going to read it after the long journey it has taken to reach you?" he asked, lifting his eyebrows in mock astonishment.

"Not now; it will keep. And I must get mother's toast and tea ready for her—there'll be barely time before father comes in to dinner."

"How is she?"

"Better, but not able to be up yet. These bad headaches always leave her weak, and I shall try to persuade her to lie still all the afternoon."

With the last word, Mildred hurried away to the kitchen.

The morning had been a very trying one. It was Monday, the day of the week on which Celestia Ann always insisted upon doing the family washing without regard to the state of the weather. She prided herself on getting her clothes out early and having them white as the driven snow, and her temper was never proof against the trial of a Monday morning storm.

There had been a steady pour of rain since before daybreak, and the queen of the kitchen was consequently in anything but an amiable mood. A severe headache had kept Mrs. Keith in bed, and to Mildred had fallen the task of guiding and controlling the domestic machinery and seeing that its wheels ran smoothly.

She had had several disputes to settle between Ada and Zillah on the one side and the irate maid-of-all-work on the other. There was also much ado to induce the younger children to attend to their lessons and then to keep them amused and quiet so that her mother might not be disturbed by their noise. Through it all, her heart was heavy with its own peculiar burden. Atmospheric influences had their depressing effect upon her spirits and upon those of the others, and more than once a sharp or impatient word, repented of as soon as uttered, had escaped her lips.

"An undeserved blessing," was her remorseful thought at sight of the letter. "It may be ill news, to be sure—oh, if it should!—yet anything is better than this terrible suspense."

But that must be borne until she could snatch a moment of solitude in which to end it.

Zillah, stooping over the kitchen fire, looked up hastily as her sister entered. "You've come to get mother's dinner, Milly? Well, here it is, all ready," she said, pointing to the teapot steaming on the hearth and beside it a plate of nicely browned and buttered toast.

"Oh, dear, good girls!" was Mildred's response as she glanced from the stove to the table, upon which Ada was placing a neatly arranged tea tray.

"As if it wasn't the greatest pleasure in the world to do a little for mother!" exclaimed the latter half indignantly. "You needn't think, Milly, that the rest of us don't love her just as well as you do."

"I meant no such insinuation," Mildred said, half laughing. "I'm sure our mother deserves the greatest possible amount of love and devotion from all her children. But may I claim the privilege of carrying up the dinner you two have prepared?"

"Yes; I suppose it's no more than fair to let you do that much, but you needn't expect me to think it's any great goodness," Ada answered, putting the finishing touches to her work and stepping aside to let Mildred take possession of the tray.

"Certainly nothing is farther from my thoughts than claiming credit for any service done to mother," Mildred answered good-humoredly as she took up the tray and walked away with it.

With quick steps she passed up the stairs, and entering her mother's room with almost noiseless tread, was greeted with a smile.

"I am not asleep, dear; and the pain is nearly gone," Mrs. Keith said, speaking from the bed in low, quiet tones.

"I am so glad, mother, and I hope a cup of tea will complete the cure," Mildred answered softly, setting down her burden on a little stand by the bedside and gently assisting her mother to a sitting position.

"A dainty little meal! My dear child, you are the greatest comfort to me!" Mrs. Keith remarked presently as she handed back the empty cup.

"But it was Zillah and Ada who prepared it today,

mother," Mildred returned, ever careful to give others their just due, though her eyes shone.

"Yes, they are dear girls, too," the mother said. "I am greatly blessed in my children, but I was thinking more of the freedom from care given me by having you here to take the head of affairs. The others, though doubtless equally willing, are still too young for that. So I could never give myself up to the full enjoyment of a headache while you were away," she added in her own peculiarly pleasant, sportive tone and manner.

"I cannot half fill your place, mother dear. I have not half your wisdom or patience," Mildred said with a blush and sigh.

"You exaggerate my virtues, Milly. I can imagine from past experience how your patience may have been tried today. Well, dear, if there has been a partial failure, do not let that rob you of our peace. 'Like as a father pitieth his children, so the Lord pitieth them that fear Him,' and though He cannot look upon sin with any degree of allowance, yet when we turn from it with true repentance and desire after holiness, pleading the merits of His dear Son as our only ground of acceptance, we find Him ever ready to forgive. What a blessing, what a glorious privilege it is that we have, in that we may turn in heart to Him for pardon and cleansing the moment we are conscious of sin in thought, word, or deed!"

"Yes, mother; I do feel it so. And how strangely kind He often is in sending joys and comforts when we feel that we deserve punishments instead,"

Mildred said with a tears springing to her eyes, as she drew out her letter and held it up.

"From Charlie!" Mrs. Keith exclaimed with a pleased smile. "My darling, I am very glad for you. I hope it brings good news."

Mildred turned it in a way to show that the seal was not yet broken, answering in low, tremulous tones, and between a smile and a sigh, "I have not found out yet. It must wait for a quiet after-dinner half-hour."

My brave, patient girl," Mrs. Keith said tenderly, passing a hand caressingly over Mildred's hair and cheek. "Let mother share the joy or sorrow, whichever it brings."

Mildred brought but scant appetite to the meal, which seemed to her an unusually long and tedious one, but she was able to control her impatience and give due attention to the comfort of father, brothers, and sisters, until at length she found herself at liberty to retire for a season to the privacy of her own room.

Her hand trembled and her heart beat fast between hope and fear as she drew the letter from her pocket and broke the seal. What if it brought ill news—that Charlie was in trouble, or that his love had grown cold? Had she strength to bear it?

Oh, not of herself! But there was One who had said, "In me is thine help." "Fear thou not, for I am with thee; be not dismayed, for I am thy God. I will strengthen thee; yea, I will help thee."

"One moment's silent pleading of His gracious promises, and she had grown calm and strong to endure whatever His providence had sent. Tears dropped upon the paper as she read, for Charlie was indeed in sore trouble. The first few sentences read as though the writer were half frenzied with distress.

He had lost everything. Both his own and his uncle's property had been suddenly and completely swept away, and the shock had killed the old gentleman—his only near relative—leaving him friendless and alone in the world. Utterly alone, utterly friendless, for he could not hope that she who had refused him in prosperity would be willing to share his poverty. Nor could he ask it. But never, never could he forget her, never could he love another.

Then under a later date, and in apparently calmer mood, he wrote:

"I am about to leave the home of my childhood and youth. It passes today into the hands of strangers, and I go out into the wide world to seek some way of retrieving my broken fortunes. With youth, health and strength, and a liberal education, surely I need not despair of finally attaining that end, though it will doubtless take years of toil and struggle. But when it is accomplished, you shall hear from me again! Nay, you shall find me at your feet, suing for the priceless boon I have hitherto sought in vain. I will not despair, for my heart tells me you will be true to me even through many long years of separation— if such fate has decreed us—and that in answer to your prayers, the barrier between us will one day be swept away."

"Share his poverty! Ah, would I not if I might!" Mildred cried half aloud and with a burst of tears. "What greater boon could I ask than the privilege of comforting him in his sorrows! Oh, Charlie, Charlie, you have given no address, and so put it out of my power to offer even the poor consolation of written words of sympathy, of hope and cheer!"

No one came to disturb Mildred in her solitude. She had time for thought and for the casting of her care upon Him who was her strong refuge, whereunto she might continually resort.

Mrs. Keith had not left her own room, and downstairs the two elder girls were busy with their needles, while Rupert kept the younger children quiet with kite-making and a story, moved thereto partly by a good-natured desire for their amusement but principally through affectionate concern for mother and elder sister.

Mrs. Keith lay on her couch, thinking a little anxiously of Mildred, when the door opened and the young girl stole softly to her side.

"Is it ill news, my darling?" the mother asked in tender, pitying accents, glancing up compassionately at the dewy eyes and tear-stained cheeks.

"I will read you his letter, mother. You know I have no secrets from you, my beloved and only confidante," Mildred answered, stopping to press a kiss on her mother's cheek.

Seating herself, she unfolded the sheet and read in low tones, which she vainly tried to make calm and even.

"Ah, mother, if only he were a Christian!" she exclaimed with a burst of uncontrollable weeping.

"Do not despair of seeing him such one day," her mother returned, laying a gentle, quieting hand on that of the weeper. "God is the hearer and answerer of prayer. The answer may be long delayed, for the trial of your faith, but it will come at last."

"What is Charlie waiting for?" sighed Mildred. "How strange that he cannot see that God's time for the sinner to come and be reconciled to Him is always now! Ah, I do so want him to know the comfort of casting all his care on the Lord—the blessedness of the man who trusts in Him!"

"Yes, it is a strange delusion! It is one of Satan's devices to persuade men to put off this most important of all transactions to a more convenient season, which he knows will never come. But, dear child, we will unite our prayers on Charlie's behalf to Him who has all power in heaven and in earth, and Who has graciously promised, 'If two of you shall agree on earth as touching anything that they shall ask, it shall be done for them of my Father which is in heaven.'"

CHAPTER XI

Ah! What is human life?
How, like the dial's tardy moving shade,
Day after day slides from us unperceiv'd!
The cunning fugitive is swift by stealth;
Too subtle is the movement to be seen;
Yet soon the hour is up—and we are gone.

—YOUNG

Mother, he seems to imply that I am not likely to hear from him again for years," Mildred said, half in assertion, half asking her mother's understanding of the drift of young Landreth's communication.

"Yes, I think so," Mrs. Keith responded in gentle tones. Then more brightly and cheerily, "But perhaps, dear, that certainty is better—will be less trying—than a constantly disappointed looking-for of letters."

Mildred gave a silent assent while a tear quickly rolled down her cheek. She dashed it hastily aside. "Mother, dearest mother, you must help me to be brave and cheerful, not letting this disappointment and anxiety spoil my life and make me a burden to myself and others," she whispered tremulously, laying her head on her mother's pillow and gazing lovingly, but through gathering tears, into those dear eyes.

113

"I will, my poor darling," returned Mrs. Keith, in moved tones, putting an arm about her daughter's neck and drawing her closer till cheek rested against cheek; "and there is One who, with all power at his command, and loving you even more tenderly than you mother does, will give you such help and consolation in this sore trial as she cannot give."

"I know it. I am sure of it," murmured Mildred. "I can trust Him for myself—though the way looks dark and dreary—but, oh, mother, it is not easy to trust for Charlie!"

"Perhaps, dear, that is one reason why this trial is sent you. Trust for our dear ones as well as for ourselves is a lesson we all need to learn."

"And to teach me patience, which is another lesson I greatly need and am very slow to learn," sighed Mildred. "'The trying of your faith worketh patience. But let patience have her perfect work.' Oh, shall I ever be able to do that?"

"Yes, at last. I am assured of it, 'being confident of this very thing, that He who hath begun a good work in you will perform it till the day of Jesus Christ.' 'In all these things we are more than conquerors through Him that loved us.' And trusting in Him, living near to Him, in the light of His countenance, we may have—we shall have—great joy and peace in spite of tribulations."

"And those I know all must have in one way or another," said Mildred a little sadly, "because we are told in Acts, 'We must through much tribulation enter into the kingdom of God.' And Jesus told his disciples, 'In the world ye shall have tribulations.'"

"But, he added, 'Be of good cheer; I have over-come the world,'" Mrs. Keith said with emotion, a joyous light shining in her eyes.

"Mother," said Mildred, "I once heard the asser-tion that God's people were peculiarly marked out for trouble and trial in this world, that they must expect to have more than was allotted to worldlings. Do you think that is true?"

"No, I find no such teaching in Scripture, nor has experience of life taught it to me. 'Many sorrows shall be to the wicked, but he that trusteth in the Lord, mercy shall compass him about.' 'Many afflictions of the righteous, but the Lord delivereth him out of them all.' 'O fear the Lord, ye His saints, for there is no want to them that fear Him!' 'Godliness is profitable unto all things, having promise of the life that now is, and of that which is to come.' The Bible is full of the blessedness of those who fear and trust the Lord."

"'Whom the Lord loveth he chasteneth, and scour-geth every son whom He receiveth,'" quoted Mildred doubtfully.

"Ah, yes; the afflictions of the righteous are the loving discipline of a tender Father, while upon the incorrigibly wicked He pours out His fury in judg-ments that bring no healing to their souls—only ret-ribution for the sins unrepented of and unforgiven. 'Upon the wicked He shall rain snares, fire and brimstone, and a horrible tempest. This shall be the portion of their cup.'"

The door opened, and Ada looked cautiously in.

"That is right, dear," Mrs. Keith said, greeting the child with a loving smile. "Come in and give mother a kiss. The pain is quite gone, and I am going to get up now and dress for tea."

"Don't, mother, unless you feel quite, *quite* strong and well," the little girl entreated, receiving and returning a tender caress. "I'm so glad you are better (oh, it isn't nice to have to do without mother, though I'm sure Milly has tried her very best to fill your place). I wouldn't have come here—because I was afraid of disturbing you—but there's a boy downstairs asking if Milly will go and watch tonight with a sick woman, Mrs. Martin. Claudina Chetwood's to watch, but there ought to be two, he says, and they don't know of anybody else for tonight. She's been sick so long that 'most everybody is worn out."

Professional nurses were unknown in the town, and in times of sickness the only dependence for needed attention, outside of the sufferer's own family, was upon the kindness of neighbors, and as a rule they were exceeding kind.

Mrs. Martin's health had been declining for many months. For weeks she had been confined to bed and in a condition to need constant watching and waiting upon.

The Keiths had scarcely a speaking acquaintance with her, but that made no difference when help was needed.

"Do you feel equal to the task, Mildred?" asked her mother. "I shall be sorry to have you lose your night's rest, but you can make it up tomorrow. I am not likely to have a return of the headache, and when I am 'to the fore' you can be spared, you know," she

116

added sportively and with a world of motherly pride and affection in the look she bent upon her firstborn.

"Yes, mother, it will not hurt me, and I can't hesitate when duty seems so plain," Mildred answered cheerfully. "How soon do they want me, Ada?"

"He says about nine o'clock. Mrs. Prior's going to stay till then. I'll go down and tell him they may expect you." And with the last word, Ada left the room.

Mrs. Keith had left the bed for a low seat before her dressing table, and Mildred was softly brushing out and arranging her still beautiful and abundant hair, very tenderly careful lest too rude a touch cause a return of the torturing pain.

"Poor, poor woman!" sighed Mrs. Keith, thinking of Mrs. Martin.

"Is she considered very dangerously ill, mother?" asked Mildred.

"Mrs. Prior was telling me about her yesterday," Mrs. Keith answered. "Dr. Grange says she had not long to live, but the worst of all, Milly, she is dying without hope."

"Oh, mother, how terrible! And has no one tried to lead her to Jesus? Has no one told her of His great love and His power and willingness to save?"

"Yes, months ago, while she was still up and about her house, Mrs. Prior and others tried to talk to her about her soul's salvation, but she refused to listen, angrily telling them she was too weak to trouble herself with trying to think on that subject now and must wait until she grew stronger—and all the time growing weaker and weaker. My child, I'm glad you are to be with her tonight, for who knows but you may find a fitting moment in which you may speak a word that God may bless to the saving of her soul."

"How glad I should be to do it," Mildred answered with emotion, "but I am so young and foolish and ignorant! Mother, how can I hope to succeed where older and wiser people have failed?"

"'Not by might, nor by power, but by my Spirit, saith the Lord of hosts.'" He often works by the feeblest instrumentalities and may see fit to use even you, my dear girl. Ask His help and His blessing upon your effort, remembering His promise, 'If any of you lack wisdom, let him ask of God, that giveth to all men liberally and upbraideth not, and it shall be given him.'"

"I will watch for an opportunity, and you will help me with your prayers, mother?"

"You may be sure of that, dear child."

"But, mother, how very much better you could speak to her than I!"

"I doubt it, Milly, for the work must be of God or it will come to naught. He can as readily make use of your mind and tongue as of mine. Don't rely on yourself; don't forget that you are only an instrument."

In spite of a very honest and earnest determination to be cheerful under this new trial of her faith and patience, and to bear her own burden according to the scriptural command, Mildred seemed to her father a little sad-eyed and paler than her wont as he looked at her across the tea table.

"My child," he said, "I hear you are expecting to watch with the sick tonight, but really, I'm afraid you are not able to do so. You do not look well."

"Appearances are sometimes deceitful, you know, father," she returned, making an effort to be bright and lively. "I am quite well, and if fatigued tonight can rest and sleep tomorrow."

"Well," he said, only half convinced, "lie down until it is time for you to go."

"Yes, Mildred, if you can get an hour or two of sleep before your watch begins, it will be a great help," said her mother. "We will call you at nine."

"Half-past eight, if you please, mother. I want to be there in time to ask directions of Mrs. Prior before she leaves."

Mildred was not sorry to seek the quiet and solitude of her own room, but she scarcely slept. She seemed to have just fallen into a doze when Rupert knocked at her door to say that it was ten minutes of the time she had for starting, and he was ready to see her to her destination.

"I'm glad you came early," was Mrs. Prior's greeting, "for indeed I ought to be at home seeing to things there. They're pretty sure to go to sixes and sevens when I'm away, and even if my boarders don't growl about it, 'tain't treatin' 'em exactly fair. But I'll not leave you alone with her. Claudina'll be here directly, and I'll stay till she comes."

"Oh, thank you!" Mildred said. "I shouldn't like to be left alone with anyone who is so ill, and I shall need to be told just what I'm to do. How is she now?"

"Can't last much longer, poor thing," Mrs. Prior returned with a sad shake of the head. "She's dreadful weak and short o' breath, and awful afraid to go. Dear, dear, to think of anybody putting off preparation to the last minute when they know they've got to die, and after that the judgment! And she won't allow a minister to come into the house, or let anybody say a word to her about her soul. Several has tried; I have myself, but it's no use. Perhaps if she'd been approached in the right way at first, it might have been different. Damaris Drybread was the first, I believe, to say anything to her, and between you and me, though Damaris means well, she's not always over-wise in her way of doing what she considers her duty. But there! I must run back to her. She oughtn't to be left alone a minute. Come into the sitting room and take off your wraps."

"The door into the next room, where the invalid lay, was open, and Mildred could hear her moaning and complaining in hollow, despairing tones, Mrs. Prior answering in cheerful, soothing accents.

Presently Mrs. Prior stepped back to the door and beckoned Mildred in.

"This is Miss Keith, Mrs. Martin," she said. "She and Miss Chetwood will watch with you tonight and do all they can to make you comfortable."

"Yes, you're all very kind. I know you'd help me if you could, but nobody can give me a minute's ease, and nobody knows what I have to suffer," moaned the sick woman, gazing piteously into the fresh young face bending over her.

Mildred's eyes filled with tears, and she opened her lips to speak but was stopped by a hasty exclamation: "Hush! Don't say a word! Don't talk to me! Don't ask me any questions! I won't hear it! I can't bear it! I'm too weak."

"I can only pray for her," was Mildred's thought as she turned sorrowfully away and hastened to the outer door, where some one had rapped lightly.

It was Claudina, and after giving them the necessary instructions, Mrs. Prior left them to their melancholy duty.

As there was not more to be done than one could easily attend to, she had advised them to take turns in watching and sleeping. There was a lounge in the sitting room where one might rest very comfortably. Claudina stretched herself on it and almost immediately fell asleep, Mildred having chosen the first watch.

The latter established herself in the sick room in an armchair by the bedside. She had brought a book, but the night lamp did not give sufficient light for reading.

Mildred had never felt wider awake, so strangely, fearfully solemn it seemed to sit there alone, waiting the coming of the angel of death to one who shuddered and shrank at his approach. Again and again while the dying woman slept, her watcher knelt by the bedside and poured out fervent though silent petitions on her behalf—and for Charlie, too, for her thoughts were full of him as well. And oh, at that moment it seemed a small matter that they might never meet on earth, could she only have the blessed assurance that eternity would unite them in another and better world.

"What's that you're doing?" asked the patient, waking suddenly. "Oh, I'm in awful distress! Rub me with some of that liniment, won't you?"

Mildred complied, doing her best to give relief to the physical suffering and crying mightily in her heart to the Great Physician for the healing of the sin-sick soul.

Oh, the distress and anguish in those hollow, sunken eyes and expressed in every lineament of the wasted features!

The bony hand clutched wildly at Mildred's dress and drew her down close, while the pale lips gasped, "I'm dying, and I'm not prepared! But I can't think — I'm too weak. I must wait till I get stronger."

"Oh, no, no! Come now to Jesus! He waits with open arms to receive you," cried Mildred, the tears coursing down her cheeks. "He died to save you, and He is able and willing to save to the uttermost all who come to Him. Come now."

"Too late, too late! I'm too weak! I can't think! Don't talk to me any more."

Mildred's ear barely caught the faintly breathed words, and with the last, the hollow eyes closed, whether in sleep she could not tell.

She found herself growing very weary, and the hands of the clock pointed to a half-hour past the set time for her vigil. She stole softly into the next room, roused Claudina, and took her place.

Her last thought as she fell into a dreamless slumber was a prayer for the two for whom she had been so importunately pleading.

She had not slept more than a moment when a hand was laid on her shoulder, and Claudina's voice, trembling with fright, said, "Mildred, Mildred! Oh, Mildred, she's gone!"

"Who?" she asked, starting up only half awake.

"Mrs. Martin. I was rubbing her, and she moaned out, 'I'm too weak. I can't think. I must wait till I'm stronger,' and with the last word, she turned her head, gasped once, and was gone."

Claudina shuddered and hid her face. "Oh, Mildred," she whispered, "those words of our Saviour are ringing in my ears: 'What shall it profit a man if he shall gain the whole world and lose his own soul?' As a girl, her head was full of dress and beaux and having a good time; as a married woman, it was keeping the best table, the neatest house, and helping her husband to get on in the world. She had no time to think about her soul until sickness came, and then she said she was too weak, she must wait to grow stronger."

They clasped each other's hands and wept silently.

Presently there was a sound of someone moving about the kitchen. "The girl's up," said Claudina, rising from her kneeling posture beside the lounge. "I'll go and tell her, and she'll let Mr. Martin know. Oh, the poor motherless baby!"

She left the room, and Mildred, starting up, saw through the crack at the side of the window-blind that the sun had risen and Mrs. Prior was at the door, come to inquire how the sick woman was.

Through the sweet morning air, pure and bracing after yesterday's showers, Mildred walked home, full of solemn, anxious thoughts: Charlie was a wanderer, she knew not where, his absorbing desire and anxiety to retrieve his broken fortunes. "Oh, that he would seek first the kingdom of God and His righteousness!" Henceforward that should be the burden of her prayer for him, for herself, and for all her dear ones.

Then her heart was filled with a great thankfulness for the spared lives of all these. Some of them had already made preparation for that last, long journey which, sooner or later, every son and daughter of Adam must take, and to the others time was still given.

CHAPTER XII

Awake in me a truer life,
A soul to labor and aspire!
Touch thou my mortal lips, O God!
With thine own truth's immortal fire.

—SARA J. CLARE

Yes, it was joy and gladness just to be alive this sweet spring morning. The swift-flowing river gleamed and sparkled in the sunlight; the forest trees on the farther side were touched with a tender yellow green; the grass along the wayside and in the dooryards was of a deeper, richer hue, and spangled thickly with violets and dandelions; and the peach and cherry trees in the gardens were in full bloom. The air was filled with fragrance, and with the twittering of birds, the ripple of the water, and other pleasant rural sounds.

The music of glad young voices came pleasantly to Mildred's ear as she reached her father's gate. Fan and Annis, who had been stooping over the flower beds, came bounding to meet her with a joyous greeting.

"How is mother?" was her first question.

"Well. She's downstairs in the sitting room cutting out sewing work."

"Yes, she's sure to be busy," Mildred said, hurrying into the house, bidding good morning to Ada, who was sweeping the front porch.

Everyone was busy with a cheerful, energetic activity. Zillah was preparing breakfast while Celestia Ann put out her clothes to dry, Rupert milked the cow, and the younger boys fed the chickens.

"Mother, you're so early at work after your sickness yesterday!" Mildred said in a tone of affectionate remonstrance as she entered the sitting room.

"Yes, daughter dear, there is need, and I am quite able for it," Mrs. Keith answered, looking up with a cheery smile. "And you are not looking so worn and jaded as I feared to see you. Did you get some sleep? And how is the poor sick woman?"

"Yes, ma'am, I slept several hours and am feeling pretty well. Mrs. Martin died about half an hour ago—very suddenly at the last. Claudina was with her. I was asleep."

Mildred's eyes filled and her voice was husky with emotion as she told of the solemn event.

A silent shake of the head was the only answer she could give to her other's next question, whether the dying woman had given any evidence that she was putting her trust in Christ.

A look of sadness and pain came over the face of the Christian mother while her heart sent up a fervent prayer on behalf of her dear ones, that each of them might be found at last hidden in the Rock of Ages.

"My child," she said to Mildred, "let us look upon this sad event as a solemn warning to us to be more faithful and constant in the work of striving to win souls to Christ, remembering that 'the night cometh, when no man can work.' Can I be sure that I am utterly guiltless of the blood of this woman to whom I never spoke one word of warning or entreaty?"

"Mother, don't blame yourself!" cried Mildred in almost indignant surprise. "You had not even a speaking acquaintance with her."

"But, my dear, I might have been. I could easily have found some excuse for calling upon her in her sickness, had I not allowed myself to be too much taken up with other cares and duties."

"But you can't do everything and take care of everybody," said Mildred with affectionate warmth; "and you are always at some good and useful work. It is I who ought to take the lesson to heart. And God helping me, I will," she added, in low, earnest, trembling tones. "Oh, mother, I feel this morning that things of this world are as nothing compared with those of the next, and I want to show by my life that I do feel so! I want to spend it wholly in the Master's service, particularly in winning souls, for—oh, the awful thought of one being lost!"

That these were no idle, lightly spoken words was proven, as days, weeks, and months rolled on, by the ever-growing consistency of Mildred's daily walk and conversation, her constant effort to bring her daily life into conformity to the divine precept, "Whether therefore ye eat or drink, or whatsoever ye do, do all to the glory of God," and that other, "As we have therefore opportunity, let us do good unto all men, especially unto them who are of the household of faith."

The members of the home circle were the first to feel the change in Mildred. She could hardly have made herself more helpful than she had long been, but her cheerfulness was more uniform, and the younger ones found her more patient with their shortcomings, more ready with sympathy and help in their little trials and perplexities. They soon learned to carry them to her as readily as to their best and kindest of mothers. They thought their eldest sister very wise and liked to consult her about their plans. This gave her many an opportunity to influence them for good, and very rarely was it neglected.

Spring was a very busy season with them all. Inside, there was housecleaning and a vast amount of sewing—so many new garments to be made, so many old ones to be renovated and altered to suit the increased stature of the growing lads and lasses. Outside, there was the gardening, the making everything neat and trim, and the care of the poultry.

Lessons were intermitted for two or three weeks to give the older members of the family time for the unusual labors while the children reveled in the delights of digging, planting, and sowing, looking after their setting hens and tending their broods of little chicks. There was a great deal of healthful pleasure gotten out of the little plots of ground appropriated to Cyril, Don, Fan, and Annis, and hardly less from their fowl. Besides, the young owners were learning habits of industry and thrift, and also the enjoyment of being able to give to the Lord's cause of that which had cost them something.

A beggar was a thing almost unknown in the town, and there were very few people poor enough to be objects of charity. But it was nice, the children thought, to have something of their very own to put into the church or Sabbath school collection, especially when it was to go to buy Bibles and pay for sending missionaries to the poor benighted heathen.

The cause of missions was dear to the hearts of the parents, and they were training their children to love and work for it.

Rupert was the principal gardener and manager of outdoor matters. He had full charge of the fruit and vegetable garden on his father's ground, and it flourished under his care. But not content with that, he had his own lot and Mildred's—which he undertook to cultivate upon shares—plowed up, then sowed with corn, potatoes, and melons.

He had his mother's talent for system and making the best use of every spare moment. An early riser, industrious, energetic, and painstaking, he managed to do all this without neglecting his studies, in preparation for college, which he was still pursuing with Mr. Lord.

He even found time for setting out trees and shrubs and digging up the flower beds in the front and side yards, doing all the hard work needed there, then giving them into the care of his mother and the older girls, who contrived to spare to the pleasing task an occasional half-hour morning and evening, finding it a rest from almost constant toil with the needle.

Cheerfully busy as Mildred was from morning to night, Charlie was seldom absent from her thoughts.

She followed him in imagination through all his wanderings, the unbidden tears often springing to her eyes as she dwelt upon the loneliness and hardships he was doubtless called to endure. Her only comfort was that she might constantly plead for him with that almighty Friend who knew it all and was ever near to both herself and her loved one.

She hoped, she prayed, that Charlie might be restored to her, with the barrier to their union removed, but most of all, that whether she should ever see him again on earth or not, he might inherit eternal life.

Her father and mother, Rupert, and Zillah were the only members of the family who knew anything of the matter. The others never so much as suspected that their bright, kind, helpful, sympathizing sister Milly was burdened with a secret sorrow or care.

Nor did she make a confidante of Claudina Chetwood, Lu Grange or Effie Prescott, though she was on intimate terms with all three.

Effie's health had improved since the Keiths first made her acquaintance, but she was still feeble and often ailing. She was a girl of fine mind, very fond of reading, and very thankful to these good neighbors for their kindness in lending her books and periodicals. And she greatly enjoyed a chat with Mrs. Keith or Mildred, for which the borrowing and returning afforded frequent occasion.

She came in one morning while they were hard at work over the pile of spring sewing.

"Good morning, ladies. Don't let me disturb you," she said as Zillah dropped her work and rose hastily to find a chair. "I see you are very busy, and I came to ask if you would let me help. I should enjoy spending the morning chatting with you all and might just as well work while I talk. And I have brought my thimble," she said, taking it from her pocket as she spoke.

"That is a very kind offer, Miss Effie, and we will be glad to have you. Take yon easy chair and chat with us as long as you will," Mrs. Keith said with her pleasant smile; "but that, I think, will be quite sufficient exertion after your walk."

"Yes, indeed, you must get quite enough of sewing at home," said Zillah. "It takes so many, many stitches to make even one garment, and lots of garments to clothe a family at all respectably."

"Yes," said Effie in a sprightly tone, "but I am fond of my needle and can use it without injury. Mildred, I see you are working buttonholes—my especial pride and delight. Won't you hand that waist to me and find something else to occupy your fingers?"

"Do you like to make them?" asked Mildred in a tone of genuine surprise. "It is my perfect detestation; therefore, I find myself sorely tempted to accept your generous offer."

Before Mildred's sentence was completed, the work had exchanged hands, Effie taking playfully forcible possession.

"My dear girl, you have a real genius for the business!" Mildred exclaimed presently. "How rapidly and nicely you work them! Two done in less time than I should take for one without doing it half so well."

Effie's eyes sparkled. "Generous praise, Mildred,"

she said, "but you can well afford to allow me the credit of doing one little thing better than you do it."

"I daresay there may be many others in which you excel me."

"No, I don't believe there's any other. And, oh, when I hear you play the piano, I feel as if I'd give anything in the world if I could play even half as well."

"Would you like to take lessons?"

"Would I!" cried Effie with emphasis. "But, dear me, there's no use thinking of it, as I'm not likely ever to have the chance."

"I'd rather give a music lesson any day than work buttonholes," remarked Mildred laughingly. "And oh, the quantities of them to be made in this family! Effie, why shouldn't we exchange work occasionally?—an hour of instruction on the piano for an hour's sewing? Don't you think it would do, mother?"

"Capitally, if you are mutually satisfied."

Effie's face was sparkling with delight. "Oh, do you really mean it?" she cried. "Why, I'd gladly give two hours' sewing for one of music lesson, and I am sure it would be worth it."

"No," said Mildred, "I think not, considering what a swift and neat needlewoman you are."

"Not much worldly wisdom in either of you, I think, my dear girls," remarked Mrs. Keith with an amused smile.

"But there's a difficulty I had not thought of," said Effie. "I have no piano to practice on."

"You shall have the use of mine."

"Thank you. I gladly accept your kind offer, if I may pay for that also with my needle."

Effie spent the day with her friends and before leaving had come to an arrangement with Mildred that was perfectly satisfactory to both, and had taken her first lesson.

Just at its close, before the two had left the piano, Claudina and Lu came in, and, hearing what Mildred had undertaken, earnestly begged that she add them to her class.

"Father is very anxious for me to learn," said Claudina, "and was wondering, the other day, if it would do to ask you to take me as a scholar. He said you could set your own price; he'd willingly pay it. But as you have no need to make money for yourself, he was afraid to propose it. Now, Milly dear, would you be offended? Of course we should feel that you were doing us a favor, even though you let us pay for it."

"No; I don't feel at all offended," Mildred said, laughing and blushing, "and I'd be glad to do anything in my power to gratify you girls or your fathers, but I really haven't time."

"Then I suppose we'll have to give it up," remarked Lu with a sigh. "But I do wish this town could afford a music teacher, for I've set my heart on learning to play."

When spring housecleaning and sewing are done, you won't be so busy, Milly," suggested Claudina.

"Yes, very nearly if not quite as busy as now, for then I take up my governessing again."

"You're the best sister and daughter I ever heard of," was Claudina's comment.

Tea was over, and Mrs. Keith stepped out to the kitchen for a consultation with Celestia Ann on the all-important subject of tomorrow's breakfast and dinner. Returning to the sitting room, she found her three girls again plying their needles.

"Come, come, my dears, no more work tonight," she said. "You, Zillah and Ada, may help me set everything to rights here so that we can go on promptly in the morning, and Mildred, child, if you are not too tired, let your father have some music. It is restful and cheering to him after his day's work and worry at the office."

"I'm never too tired to play for father or mother," Mildred said with a smile as she rose to do her mother's bidding.

"There! Don't wait to fold that; I'll do it," Zillah said, taking the work from her hand. "And, mother, please go into the parlor and rest yourself in the big rocking chair and leave this clearing up to Ada and me."

"Yes, mother, please do," chimed in the younger girl. "We'd a great deal rather, and you know we can just as well as not."

"Thank you, dears; then I will. What comforts and blessings you are to me—all three of you!"

"Me too, mother?—me and Fan?" asked little Annis, following and standing beside her mother's chair with an eager, upturned face and pleading eyes.

"Yes, indeed, darling! Mother wouldn't know how to do without her baby girl or her dear little Fan," Mrs. Keith answered, lifting the one into her lap and drawing the other close to her side, for Fan, too, had followed her in from the sitting room.

"I'm not of much use yet, mother, 'cept to love you," she said, nestling closer, "but I'm going to be some day, if I live. See! I've hemmed one side o' this handkerchief, and didn't I make nice bits of stitches?" she asked, holding it up for inspection.

"Yes, indeed, darling, I can see that you have taken great pains. Why, I think after a while I shall have no need to sew at all, with so many fingers to do the work. Go and show it to your father."

Fan obeyed, was praised, caressed, and taken upon her father's knee, where she sat in quiet content listening to Mildred's music.

Presently, Squire Chetwood was ushered in by Celestia Ann.

"Go on, Miss Mildred," he said as he took the seat Mr. Keith hastened to offer. "There's no greater treat for me than your music, and my errand will keep for a bit."

It proved, when told, one that rejoiced them all. It was to show Mr. Keith a letter of acceptance from a gentleman teacher with whom they had been corresponding with a view to securing his services as principal of a school that they were trying to establish in the town. It was to be for both sexes, and the gentleman's wife would take charge of the girl's department.

"I send four pupils — Zillah, Ada, Cyril, and Don," said Mr. Keith, "thereby considerably lightening your labors, wife, and Mildred's, too, I trust."

The squire cleared his throat. "And then, Miss Mildred — ah, I hardly dare go on lest you should think me presuming!"

"But after exciting my curiosity, you can hardly refuse to gratify it," Mildred returned playfully, though she knew very well what was coming.

Before the squire went away she had consented to take another music scholar, and the terms he offered were very liberal, she having declined to name a price for her services.

"Having accepted Claudina, you can hardly refuse Lu," her mother remarked when the squire had gone.

"No, mother, and how little time I shall have left for helping you!" sighed Mildred.

"Now, Milly, don't try to make yourself out to be of so much importance!" cried Zillah in a merry, bantering tone. "Didn't mother do without you entirely last year? One would suppose Ada and I were of no consequence where work is concerned."

"But you will be in school, child!"

"Not for the first four hours after we leave our beds in the morning, or the last four or five before we return to them at night."

"Besides an hour or more at noon," added Ada. "And if we can't do something to help mother in all that time, we'll deserve to be called lazy girls."

"We shall do nicely, I am sure," the mother said with a pleased, loving glance at each of the three faces in turn. "I think we can manage so that everything will be attended to and no one of us overworked. I can easily hear Fan's and Annis's little lessons every day while sewing. Your five music scholars, Mildred, will occupy only ten hours a week of your time, while one of them will do an hour's sewing for you every day and the other two outsiders will bring you in a nice little sum of pocket money."

"Why, it doesn't look so very laborious after all!" Mildred said, brightening.

"No," laughed Zillah, "you could take half a dozen more music scholars and not be hurt."

CHAPTER XIII

Wouldst thou from sorrow find a sweet relief,
Or is thy heart oppress'd with woes untold?
Balm wouldst thou gather for corroding grief,
Pour blessings round thee like a shower of gold!

—CARLOS WILCOX

Mildred's charity, beginning at home, did not end there. Very earnestly and persistently, she strove to scatter blessings as "a shower of gold" wherever she went, to make every life that came in contact with hers, at ever so small a point, the better and brighter for that contact, though it were by but a cheery word or smile.

Do you say these are small matters, scarcely worthy of attention? Ah, to each of us comes the divine command, "Be pitiful, be courteous," and the Master said of the tithing of mint, anise, and cumin, while the weightier matters of the law were neglected, "These ought ye to have done, and not to leave the other undone." "He that is faithful in that which is least, is faithful also in much."

It was so with Mildred. Never considering herself off duty as a Christian soldier, she was as ready to feed the hungry, clothe the naked, teach the ignorant, and nurse the sick as to bestow the kind word and pleasant smile that cost her nothing. Nothing? Ah, there were times of weariness and depressions when even these trifles cost a heroic effort—a determined setting aside of selfish inclination to moodiness or irritability, or indulgence in a pleasing melancholy, because one great earthly blessing was denied her.

In this her bright, cheerful mother, always ready with a word of counsel and encouragement, was a wonderful help. Indeed, by frequent precept and constant example Mrs. Keith succeeded in making all her children, to a greater or lesser degree, sunny-tempered and benevolent, kind and courteous.

The Dorcas society connected with their church had no more active, efficient, or liberal members than this good lady and her eldest daughter. In proportion to their ability, they gave freely of time, labor, and money. They were, indeed, always found ready to every good work, though they trusted not in their works for acceptance in the sight of God but only in the atoning blood and imputed righteousness of Christ. "Followers of God as dear children," theirs was a service of love and joy, rendered not that they might *be* saved but because they *were* saved.

Questions of doctrine and duty were freely discussed in the family circle, the children bringing them in all confidence to their parents for decision, and the parents always appealing to the Scriptures as the one infallible rule of faith and practice—as they are in very truth.

"To the law and to the testimony, if they speak not according to this word, it is because there is no light in them." "For the commandment is a lamp, and the law is the light."

One Sabbath a returned missionary preached in the morning to Mr. Lord's congregation and in the afternoon addressed the assembled Sunday schools of the town.

The Keiths came home from the latter service very full of what they had heard of the sad condition of the heathen world, the need for money to carry on the work of evangelizing them, and the self-denying efforts some of God's children, both old and young, were making to earn and save so that they might be able to give to this good cause.

Cyril had been especially interested in the story of a little boy who had raised a pig, sold it, and had given to missions the whole of what he received for it.

"I mean to have a missionary pig," Cyril said to Don as they walked home together. "I'll take good care of it and feed it well, so it will be very fat, so that I can get ten dollars for it, and every cent of it shall go to the missionaries. And I'll make some more besides for them out of my garden and my chickens."

"So will I," said Don; "but I shan't let 'em have all the money."

"How much, then?"

"I don't know yet."

"I'm afraid it won't do for all of us to have pigs," said Ada, overhearing the talk of her little brothers.

"No," laughed Zillah, "we'd overstock the market and bring down the price."

"I don't see what I can do then, except give some of my pocket money, unless mother will pay me for doing without butter and tea and sugar, as some children do that the missionaries told about."

"That's too hard a way," said Cyril. "You won't catch me trying that. I'll work for the heathen, but I won't starve for 'em."

"It would be hard, but we ought to deny ourselves," Ada returned half regretfully.

"Yes, in some things," Zillah said. "I don't feel sure about this. We'll ask father and mother."

They did so immediately on entering the house.

"Your mother and I have just been discussing that question," Mr. Keith said, "and we think that as good, nourishing food is necessary to your health and growth, it is not a duty for you to deny yourselves such common comforts as butter and sugar. There are better ways in which to practice self-denial."

"How, father?" asked Ada.

"It might be by denying our love of ease—working and earning for the good of others, when we would rather be at play. The Bible speaks of laboring, working with our hands that we may have to give to him that needeth."

"And who is more needy than the poor, benighted heathen!" sighed Mrs. Keith.

"It won't hurt us to deny ourselves in the matter of finery," remarked Mildred.

"Or eating more than enough to satisfy our appetites, just because it tastes good," added Rupert.

"No, that is sinful in itself, because it is injurious to health," said his father.

"But haven't we a right to eat what we please and just as much as we choose, if we would rather be

sick than do without the good things, father?"
asked Cyril.

"No, my son; health is one of God's good gifts,
which we have no right to throw away. We can't
serve Him with a sick and suffering body so well as
with a strong, healthy one. And we are told in
Proverbs, 'The drunkard and the glutton shall come
to poverty.'"

"Father, does God want us to give all our money
away to other folks?" asked Don.

"No, son, not all. Our heavenly Father intends for
us to use some of it to supply our own needs."

"What proportions ought we to give, father?"
asked Rupert.

"I think that depends upon how large our means
are."

"Is not a tenth the Bible rule?" asked Mrs. Keith.

"Yes, God claims a tenth as His. It seems plain that
everyone should give that—or more properly pay it
to the Lord—and those who are able to do more
should add offerings in proportion to their ability. So
I gather from this text in Malachi, third chapter and
eighth verse." Opening a Bible, Mr. Keith read
aloud: "Will a man rob God? Yet ye have robbed me.
But ye say, 'Wherein have we robbed Thee? In tithes
and offerings.'"

"I thought that was the rule under the Levitical
law, and that the New Testament rule was 'Give as
God has prospered you,'" said Rupert.

"Yes, we are to give as God has prospered us—one
dollar out of every ten, one hundred out of every
thousand, and so on. The beginning of tithe-paying

was not in the time of Moses but hundreds of years before, for we read that Abraham paid tithes and that Jacob promised to the Lord the tenth of all that He should give him. We nowhere read that Jesus abrogated this law. Indeed, he said, 'Think not that I am come to destroy the law or the prophets; I am not come to destroy, but to fulfill' of the tithing of 'mint and rue and all manner of herbs,' that it ought not to be left undone.

"And God promises blessings, both temporal and spiritual, to those who faithfully obey this law of the tithes. 'Bring ye all the tithes into the storehouse, that there may be meat in mine house; and prove me now herewith, saith the Lord of hosts, if I will not open you the windows of heaven, and pour you out a blessing, that there shall not be room enough to receive it. And I will rebuke the devourer for your sakes, and he shall not destroy the fruits of your ground; neither shall your vine cast her fruit before the time in the field, saith the Lord of hosts.'

"'Honor the Lord with thy substance and with the first-fruits of all thine increase; so shall thy barns be filled with plenty, and thy presses shall burst out with new wine.'

"'Trust in the Lord, and do good; so shalt thou dwell in the land, and verily thou shalt be fed.'

"'There is that scattereth, and yet increaseth; and there is that withholdeth more than is meet, but it tendeth to poverty.'

"'He that hath pity upon the poor, lendeth unto the Lord; and that which he hath given will he pay him again.'

"These are not all the texts bearing on the subject, but will suffice for the present."

"Father," said Don, "God doesn't need our money, does He? Why does He tell us to give it to Him?"

"For our own good, my son. Don't you remember Jesus said, 'It is more blessed to give than to receive'? He cannot be happy who indulges a mean, sordid disposition. The less selfish we are, the more ready to help others and share our good things with them, the happier and the more like our heavenly Father we shall be. Try it, my boy, and you will find it is so. And the more constantly you practice giving, the more we shall be in love with it."

"And then shall our gifts be pleasing to God," added the mother. "'Every man according as he purposeth in his heart, so let him live; not grudgingly, or of necessity, for God loveth a cheerful giver. And God is able to make all grace abound toward you; that ye, always having all sufficiency in all things, may abound to every good work.'"

"Well, it seems, if we obey the Bible rule, we will give a tenth of our pocket money and of all we can make besides," remarked Rupert.

"And I am very glad I can earn something by teaching music," said Mildred.

"I think you can each find some way of earning something for this good purpose," the mother said, glancing smilingly around the little group.

Cyril told eagerly of his plan. Don added that he meant to have a missionary pig, too, but not to give all that he made on it.

"You must decide for yourselves whether to give more than a tenth of its price," his father said, "but I think 'missionary pig' will hardly be an appropriate name unless it is entirely devoted to the cause."

"Mother," said Fan, "wouldn't it be nice for me to call one of my hens a missionary hen and give all the money I get from her and her eggs to the heathen?"

"Yes, dear, I think it would be very nice," Mrs. Keith said, sending a loving glance into the earnest face.

"Then I'll do it, and I hope she'll lay an egg every day."

"And *I'll* have a missionary hen!" cried little Annis, clapping her hands with delight at the idea of contributing her mite to the good cause.

"Ada and I haven't matured our plans yet," said Zillah, "but we'll be sure to find some way to make money as well as the rest of you."

"Mother will help us to contrive it, won't you, mother?" Ada said, with a look of confiding affection.

The answer was a prompt, emphatic "Yes, indeed, my dear."

But Mr. Keith seemed to have something further to say, and all turned to listen.

"We want to give the missionary some money today or tomorrow to carry away with him. Who has any ready now?"

Cyril's countenance fell. He was a great spendthrift, and money slipped through his fingers almost as soon as it came into his possession.

"My pocket money's all gone," he sighed half aloud, half to himself. Nudging his younger brother, he said, "Don, you always have some; won't you lend me a little?"

"No," declared Mr. Keith, "you are not to go into debt, even from a good motive. After this, set aside the Lord's tenth of all your money as soon as it comes into your hands, and use that portion scrupulously for Him in giving to the church and the poor. And, my son, I want you to form a habit of laying by a little for your own future needs. You will be a poor man if you spend all your money as fast as you get it."

"I don't," remarked Don complacently; "I save 'most all I get."

"Ah, yes, my boy, I know that and often feel troubled about my youngest son, that he should become a hard, grasping, miserly man, loving and hoarding money for its own sake. Do you know that that is as truly idolatry as the bowing down of the heathen to images of wood and stone?"

"Is it, father?" murmured the little lad, his face crimsoning and tears starting to his eyes.

"It is indeed, Don, and so a worse fault than Cyril's foolish spending, bad as that is. The Bible bids us mortify 'covetousness, which is idolatry.'"

"Try, both of you, to save in order 'to have to give to him that needeth,' and to 'provide things honest in the sight of all men.' We must first pay to the Lord His tenth, then to our fellow men what we honestly owe them; after that, give to the needy what we feel able to spare from our store. We are not told to pull down our barns and build greater, there to bestow our surplus goods, while we take our ease, eat, drink, and be merry, and neglect to relieve the distress and suffering of the poor and needy."

"Like the rich man in the Bible?" said Fan. "Father, was he a very bad man?"

"Probably not what the world calls bad. We are not told that he was dishonest, drunken, or profane, but he was selfish and covetous — caring for the good things of this world and neglectful of eternal things. And selfishness is sin as well as covetousness. They seem to go together and shut the soul out of heaven. The Bible says, 'Nor thieves, nor covetous, nor drunkards, nor revilers, nor extortioners shall inherit the kingdom of God.'"

"I thought coveting was wanting other people's things," remarked Ada.

"That is coveting," replied her father, "and so is that inordinate love of gain, which leads men to drive hard bargains and to heap up riches at the expense of leaving those to suffer whom they are fully able to relieve. When the Lord gives us large means, it is so that, as his stewards, we may distribute to others. Well, Rupert, what is it?"

"I have the money I had saved toward buying a piano. I will give a tenth of it now."

"That is well. Who else has anything for the missionary?"

"I have a little of the pocket money Aunt Wealthy supplies," Mildred said. "I wish I could give more now. I hope to when the money comes in from my music scholars, but that will not be for some time, you know."

"I haven't much money," said Fan, "but maybe I can sell my eggs. I have a whole dozen."

"I'll give some of my money," said Don.

"And I," said Zillah and Ada together.

Mrs. Keith also promised something, and Mr. Keith added that he, too, would give, and they would collect it all and hand it to the missionary before his departure, which was to be the next afternoon.

"Father, is it right to pray for earthly prosperity?" asked Rupert.

"That depends very much upon the motive. The apostle James says, 'Ye have not, because ye ask not. Ye ask, and receive not, because ye ask amiss, that ye may consume it upon your lusts.' It is not the asking he condemns (he seems, indeed, to reprove them for not asking) but the wrong motive for so doing. Let us compare Scripture with Scripture. The Psalmist tells us, 'Except the Lord build the house, they labor in vain that build it: except the Lord keep the city, the watchman waketh but in vain. It is vain for you to rise up early, to sit up late, to eat the bread of sorrows; for so he giveth his beloved sleep.'

"In Deuteronomy we are told, 'Thou shalt remember the Lord thy God, for it is He that giveth thee power to get wealth.' Evidently we cannot attain to worldly prosperity except by God's help—his blessing on our efforts. We may work for prosperity, and we may pray for it, from either a right or a wrong motive, and certainly in either case we are approved or the contrary according to the motive that actuates us. 'Man looketh on the outward appearance, but the Lord looketh on the heart.'"

"What would be a right motive, father?" asked Ada in her grave, earnest way.

"The desire to have the ability to 'provide things honest in the sight of all men,' to help in the Lord's cause—the work of the church—and to give to the poor and needy. Many desire wealth for their own ease and indulgence, for the consequence it gives them in the eyes of their fellow men, or as a means of gaining power over them. It cannot be right to pray for it from such motives—that is the sort of asking the apostle condemns."

Mrs. Keith was turning over the leaves of the Bible. "'Let the Lord be magnified, who hath pleasure in the prosperity of his servants,'" she read aloud. "What the Lord takes pleasure in, and what He promises upon conditions, it cannot be wrong to ask for, unless from a wrong motive," she remarked. "And it is clear to my mind that if it be wrong to pray for prosperity, it is also wrong to work for it. Certainly a Christian should never engage in anything upon which he cannot ask God's blessing. But we are commanded to be 'diligent in business,' and told the 'the hand of the diligent maketh rich.'"

"Yes," said her husband, "'Not slothful in business, fervent in spirit, serving the Lord.' If we are careful not to divorce these two which God hath joined together, we need not fear to ask His blessing on our labors."

CHAPTER XV

*The whining schoolboy with his satchel
And shining morning face, creeping like a snail
Unwillingly to school.*

—SHAKESPEARE

The new school had opened the previous week and was now in successful operation. Zillah and Ada were pursuing their studies with redoubled zeal and interest, finding a constant spur in the desire to keep pace with, if not outstrip, the other members of their classes.

Mildred was often applied to for help in the home preparation of their lessons, and her assistance, always cheerfully and kindly given, was received with due appreciation.

"With such good help at home," they would say, "we ought to do better than any of the other girls, for there isn't one of them who has a sister so capable of explaining whatever in their lessons they find difficult to understand, or so willing to do it."

"I am only returning to you what mother has done for me in past days," Mildred answered more than once. "And if I did not do it, she would."

150

"Yes," was the rejoinder, "there isn't such another mother in the town—or anywhere else, for that matter."

The little boys, accustomed to passing most of the day in the open air after essaying their tasks on the porch or in the shade of the trees, found the confinement of the schoolrooms very irksome.

Mother and Mildred were frequently appealed to for sympathy in their trial, and the demand was always sure to be met with bright, hopeful, cheery words of encouragement to patience and diligence. "They must be willing to bear a little discomfort in the pursuit of the knowledge which is so important to their future success in life—must try to learn all they can, that they might grow up to be wise useful men, capable of doing God service and of helping themselves and others."

Hitherto the little fellows had been kept out of the streets and carefully shielded from the snares and temptations of association with the evil-disposed and wicked. The time for a trial of the strength of their principles had now come, and parents and elder sister looked on with deep anxiety for the result.

The perfect openness engendered in them by never-failing sympathy in all their little childish joys and sorrows, plans and purposes, now proved to be a wonderful safeguard. Why should they want to hide anything from those whose interest in and love for them was made so apparent? They did not, and so many a wrong step was avoided or speedily retrieved.

In that first week of school, Cyril had got himself into disgrace with his teacher by a liberal distribution among his mates of gingerbread and candy, for which he had spent his whole store of pocket money.

The good things were carried into the schoolroom, the master's attention drawn to them by the constant munching and crunching among the boys.

A search was promptly instituted, the remainder of the feast confiscated, and an explanation called for.

"Who brought these things here?" was the stern demand.

"I, sir; I brought them and gave them to the fellows, and so I am more to blame than anybody else," Cyril said, rising in his seat and speaking out with manly courage and honesty, though his cheeks were ablaze and his heart beat fast.

"Then, sir, you shall be punished with the loss of your recess and being kept in for an hour after school," was the stern rejoinder. "I will have no such doings here."

There was not a word of commendation of the boy's moral courage and readiness to confess his fault, and he had to endure not only the loss of his playtime but also was severely lectured and threatened with a flogging if ever the offense should be repeated.

He went home very angry and indignant, and his mother being out, carried his grievance to Mildred. He poured out the whole story without reserve, finishing with, "Wasn't it the greatest shame for him to punish me twice for the same thing? I'm sure the loss of my recess was quite enough, 'specially considering that I owned up the minute he asked about it. And then the idea of threatening to flog me! Why, I haven't had a whipping since I was a little bit of a fellow, and I'd think it an awful disgrace to get one now that I'm so big, 'specially at school. I say nobody but father or mother has a right to touch me, and nobody shall! I'll just knock old Peacock down if he dares to try it, that I will!"

"Oh, Cyril, Cyril, you should not be so disrespectful toward the teacher father has set over you!" Mildred said, striving to speak quietly, though because of her indignation at the severity and injustice of the treatment the child had received, and the mirth-provoking idea of his imagining himself able to cope with a man, she found it no easy matter. "I'm really sorry you have wasted your money and broken the rules."

"No, I didn't!" the boy burst out hotly. "He'd never made any rule about it, though he has now, and says I ought to have known and must have known that such things couldn't be allowed."

"Well, that seems unreasonable, but I suppose you might if you had stopped to think. You know, Cyril dear, how often father and mother have urged you to try to be more thoughtful."

"Yes; but it seems as if I can't, Milly. How's a fellow to help being thoughtless and careless when it comes so natural?"

"Our wicked natures are what we have to strive against, and God will help us if we ask Him," she answered, speaking that holy name in reverent tones.

Don, who had waited about the schoolhouse door for Cyril and walked home by his side, was standing by listening to the talk. "Oh, Milly! We don't like that school!" he said, with a look of weariness and disgust. "It is so hard to have to be shut up there and obliged to sit still 'most all day long. Won't you ask father to let us stay at home and say lessons to you again?"

"Oh, yes, Milly, do!" Cyril joined in. "Fan's ever so lonesome without us, and we'll be as good as we know how, study hard, and not give you a bit of trouble."

Mildred explained that the arrangements had been made for the summer and could not now be altered.

"And surely," she concluded, with an encouraging smile, "my two little brothers are not such cowards as to be conquered by little difficulties and discomforts. Don't you know we have to meet such things all the way through life? And the best way is to meet them with a cheerful courage and determination to press on notwithstanding. 'The slothful man saith there is a lion in the way.' 'The way of the slothful man is an hedge of thorns.' Don't be like him.'"

"Does that mean that folks are lazy when they give up because things are hard?"

"Yes, Don. And if we are so ready to do that, we are not likely to get to heaven, because that is no easy matter—with our sinful hearts, a wicked world, and Satan and all his hosts to fight against. We have to 'fight the good fight of faith'—to 'lay hold on eternal life'—to 'press toward the mark for the prize of the high calling of God in Christ Jesus'—to 'run with patience the race that is set before us.' Jesus said 'The kingdom of heaven suffereth violence, and the violent take it by force.'"

"Milly, what does that mean?"

"That to get to heaven it is necessary to strive very, very earnestly and determinately."

"Milly, how can Don and I fight that fight?" asked Cyril. "Do tell us."

"Just as grown people must—by loving and trusting Jesus and striving earnestly every day and hour to serve God in doing faithfully the duty that comes nearest to hand. And don't you see that the principal part of yours at present is to be good, faithful workers at school, and obedient to your teacher, because father has given him authority over you when you are at school?"

"Yes, I 'spose so," sighed Don. "But, oh, Milly, I did want to run away this afternoon and take a nice walk 'stead of going to school. It's so nice down by the river and in the woods 'mong the birds and flowers."

"Yes, I know it is, Don, but it would have been very wrong to go without leave. And I can't tell you how glad I am that you resisted the temptation."

Now that money was wanted for the missionary, Cyril was sorry for having spent his so foolishly.

"I was very bad to waste it in that way," he said regretfully. "It was all because I didn't think. But I mean to think after this and try to make the best use of all the money I get."

The new school was nearly as great an affliction to Fan as to the little boys. She was so lonely without Cyril and Don—hitherto her inseparable companions and playmates—and now it depended upon her to run errands for her mother and sister when they were in too great haste to await the boys' leisure. Fan, being extremely timid and bashful, found this no small trial.

It was Monday morning, and the scholars were trooping into the schoolhouse—the Keiths among the rest.

At home, Mildred was in the parlor giving a music lesson, and Fan was in the sitting room waiting for mother to come and hear her read and spell.

Mrs. Keith came in and sat down at her writing desk.

"Fan, darling, mother wants you to do an errand for her," she said, taking up her pen.

"What, mother?" the child ask half plaintively.

"To carry a note for me to Mrs. Clark. I want you to take it there immediately and tell her you will wait for an answer. And then, as you come back, call at Chetwood & Mocker's and ask for a yard of calico like the piece I shall give you, and also ask how much they are selling eggs for today by the dozen. Then I will buy your dozen of you, and you will have the money for the missionary."

"Oh, mother," sighed the little girl, "I don't like to go to the store all alone, or to Mrs. Clark's either. I don't know her."

"I am sorry my dear little girl is so bashful, but that is something that must be overcome and cannot be except by refusing to indulge it. You may take Annis with you, though, if you choose."

"Thank you, mother, but Annis is so little that I'll have to do all the talking just the same."

"Well, dear, you can talk quite prettily, if you only forget to think about yourself. Try to forget little Fan Keith, and think of the messages she has to deliver, the questions she must ask, and you will find there is no trouble at all."

"Oh, mother! please let somebody else go."

Fan had put down her book, gone to her mother's side, and was standing there looking pleadingly into her face.

Mrs. Keith bent down as she folded her note and pressed a loving kiss on the child's forehead.

"My little girl will go to please mother and the dear Lord Jesus. There is no one else to go now, and the errands cannot wait for the boys to come home from school."

"Will it please Jesus, mother?"

"Yes, dear, because He bids you to honor and obey your mother and also to deny yourself when duty calls. You know one part of the errand at the store is to help you obtain the money for the poor heathen."

"Mother, I'd rather do 'most anything else for them, but I'll go to please you and the Lord Jesus. And I want Annis to go, too. Will you, Annis?"

"I guess I will! I'd like to," the little one answered joyously.

It was a busy morning for Mrs. Keith, and getting Annis ready for the walk involved some small loss of time, but she considered the pleasure she would thus give her little ones well worth the sacrifice.

"Now, Fan," she said when the children were about to start, and she put the note and sample calico into the little girl's hands, with a repetition of her com-

missions, "remember that you are the errand girl and
have all the responsibility, because Annis is too little.
But you are mother's big, useful girl, and I know you
are glad to be a help and comfort to mother."

The tender, loving words infused courage into the
timid little heart for the moment, and the two set off
with bright faces. But Fan's clouded again and her
heart beat fast as she neared Mrs. Clark's door.

Had it not been open, her timid little rap would
hardly have been heard. Her message, delivered
with the note, was given in tones so low that the lady
had to ask her to repeat it while she bent her ear to
catch the words.

At the store it was even worse. Not yet recovered
from the embarrassment of her call upon Mrs. Clark,
Fan stumbled and stammered, saaying she wanted a
dozen calicoes for her mother, and asking how much
they charged for eggs by the yard.

Then catching the mirthful gleam in Will
Chetwood's eyes and seeing the corners of his lips
twitching, she hastily withdrew into the shelter of her
sunbonnet, quite overwhelmed with confusion by the
sudden consciousness of having made a terrible blunder, her cheeks aflame and her eyes filling with tears.

"I think it is a yard of calico like that in your hand
that you want, and the price of eggs by the dozen,
isn't it?" he asked pleasantly.

"Yes, sir, that's what mother said," Annis spoke up
briskly.

Fan was quite beyond speaking and kept her face
hidden in her sunbonnet. She hurried away the
moment the little parcel was handed to her.

Mildred was alone in the sitting room as they came in.

"Where's mother?" asked Annis.

"In the parlor, talking to Mr. Lord. You got the calico, Fan? Here, give it to me." Then, catching sight of the child's face as she drew near, she asked in a tone of kindly concern, "Why, what's the matter? What have you been crying about?"

"Oh, Milly, I couldn't help it! I don't like to go on errands!" moaned Fan, bursting into tears again.

Mildred drew the little weeper to her side, wiped away her tears, kissed the wet cheeks, and with kindly questioning drew the whole story from her.

"And Mr. Chetwood was laughing at me, I know he was! I don't want ever to go there any more!" concluded the child, hiding her burning cheeks on Mildred's shoulder.

"Oh! you needn't mind that," Mildred said. "Just join in the laugh. That's the way Aunt Wealthy does, and your mistake is very much like some of hers."

"Then I don't care so much, for nobody's nicer than Aunt Wealthy—unless it's mother, father, and you."

"You needn't except me. I'm by no means equal to Aunt Wealthy," Mildred said, smiling, and stroking Fan's hair.

Annis had run into the parlor, and they were quite alone.

"Milly," said Fan, after a moment's silence, "I thought God heard our prayers."

"So He does, Fan."

"Yes, but I thought He would do what we asked."

"Not always, because we often ask for something that He sees would not be good for us. But what are you thinking about? Have you prayed for something that you didn't get? Perhaps you expected the answer too soon. We often have to wait and pray again and again many times, and at last the answer comes. And sometimes it comes in a better way than we had thought of."

"I'll tell you, Milly," Fan said slowly and hesitatingly, "I prayed that Mrs. Clark mightn't be at home; but there she was."

Mildred could scarcely keep from smiling. "That wasn't a good or right prayer, little sister," she said, "because—don't you see?—it was selfish and almost the same as disobeying mother, since if the prayer had been granted, you would have been prevented from doing her errand."

"Milly, I didn't think of that," Fan answered penitently. "I won't pray that way anymore."

"No, dear, a better prayer would be for help to overcome your foolish timidity. We will both ask our kind heavenly Father for that."

CHAPTER XVI

Whither my heart is gone,
there follows my hand and not elsewhere.

—LONGFELLOW

We will pass briefly over the events of the next five years, during which there were few changes in the Keith family but such as time must bring to all.

The lines had deepened somewhat on Mr. Keith's brow, and the hair on his temples was growing gray. The anxieties and burdens of life pressed more heavily upon him than upon his lighter-hearted, more trustful wife, she having learned more fully than he to "lean hard" upon the Lord, casting all her care upon Him in the full assurance that He cared for her and "that all things work together for good to them that love God." She looked scarcely a day older than at the time of Mildred's return from her visit to Roselands.

These had been years of toil and struggle to feed, clothe, and educate their large family of children. They had thus far been successful but only by dint of good management, close economy, and hard work.

Rupert had finished his college course and gone into the medicine business in connection with Dr. Grange.

It was a great joy to Mildred that her earnings as a music teacher had assisted largely in paying the expense of her brother's education. Rupert found it hard to consent to this but finally did so with the distinct understanding that he was to repay the money with interest. "The sisterly kindness," he said, "I can never repay."

"Yes," Mildred returned with an arch look and smile, "you can, by showing in like manner brotherly kindness to Cyril and Don."

"As I certainly hope to do," Rupert responded with hearty goodwill.

And now he and Mildred were pleasing themselves with the thought that the worst of the struggle was over. Zillah and Ada were done with school, though they were still pursuing some studies with Mildred at home. It had been decided that Fan and Annis could and should be entirely educated by their older sisters, and so Cyril and Don were the only ones whose tuition would still be an item of expense to the parents—an expense of which the good daughter and son each hoped to bear a part.

Rupert would be able to do so after awhile—"by the time the lads were ready for college"—and Mildred could assist now, as she was still teaching and finding it more profitable than ever.

It sometimes seemed weary work, but she would not give it up. Indeed, the joy of helping to bear the burdens of the dear father and mother far more than repaid her for her self-denying toil.

The town had grown very much, and one of the newcomers was a music teacher, but Mildred had established a good reputation and had always as many pupils as she cared to take.

In all these years she had not heard a word from Charlie Landreth, yet her heart remained true to him.

She did not seclude herself from society but generally took part in the innocent pastimes of the young people of her own station. She was always cheerful and pleasant, often even merry and lively. Now and then she accepted the escort of one or another of her gentlemen friends, but she would not receive particular attention from any. Still one or two had determinately sought her hand in marriage but only to meet with a gentle yet firm rejection.

Wallace Ormsby still continued on the most friendly terms of intimacy with the family, and after two years had passed without news of his favored rival, ventured to renew his suit. The result of this effort convinced him of the utter hopelessness of ever winning the coveted prize. He grieved over this second disappointment for a time but of late had begun to turn his longing eyes in a new direction, and Mildred perceived it with pleasure.

Wallace had been taken into partnership with Mr. Keith, and she would gladly welcome him into the family, for she had, as she had said, a truly sisterly affection for him.

Zillah and Ada were budding into very lovely womanhood. Of the two, Zillah was the more strikingly handsome and the more sprightly, full of innocent mirth and merriment, witty and quick at repartee. She was the life of every company of which she formed a part.

Ada's manner was more quiet and reserved but suited well her intellectual countenance and the noble contour of her features. They were inseparable, and whenever opportunity offered, Wallace Ormsby was sure to be with them.

Speculation was rife among the gossips of the town as to "which he was courting," or whether it might be that he was in love with both. Mildred, with her better opportunities for observation and vision sharpened by keen sisterly affection, presently settled that question in her own mind and satisfied herself that, in this instance, the course of true love was likely to run smooth,

The little coterie of which Mildred and Wallace had formed a part was broken up—the other four having paired off for life. It was known now that Claudina Chetwood was engaged to Yorke Mocker, and Lucilla Grange to Will Chetwood.

It was the afternoon of the ladies' sewing society meeting. They were preparing a box of clothing for a Western home missionary. The whole Keith family took a deep interest in the work, and each one had contributed toward it. The three older girls were at the meeting, busily plying their needles, while at home the mother was finishing a garment, the two little girls sitting beside her hemming towels, all for the box.

Indeed, the interest was very general in the church, and there was a goodly gathering of ladies in Mrs. Prior's parlor, where the society held its meeting this week. The room was large and the busy workers had grouped themselves together here and there as inclination dictated: Mildred, Claudina, and

Lu forming one group; Zillah, Ada and several of their young companions another; while a third was composed of the older ladies.

The three ladies in the first groups were very close together, the three voices conversing earnestly in tones too subdued to give any of the others an inkling of the subject of their talk. But there were some surmises.

"I reckon they're planning for the weddings," whispered one elderly lady to her next neighbor, indicating by a motion of the head whom she meant.

"Likely," was the rejoinder. "Do you know when they're to come off?"

"No, but before long, I guess. I don't see that there's anything to wait for."

"Unless for Mildred and Wallace Ormsby to make it up together, so that the whole six can pair off at once and so make a triple wedding. It would be a novel and pretty idea, now wouldn't it?"

"Yes, and I used to think that would be a match, but I've changed my mind. It's plain to be seen now that it's one of the younger sisters he's after."

"Mildred's young enough, doesn't look a day over twenty, though I suppose she's really twenty-three or -four."

"About that, I suppose, but she could easily pass for eighteen. I wonder if she's made up her mind to be an old maid. If I can read the signs, Wallace was deeply in love with her at one time, and it's said she's had other offers."

"I don't doubt it. She's too charming to have escaped that, if the young men have any taste. Yet she's not so handsome, after all, as Zillah. I wonder why she wouldn't have Wallace. He's fine-looking and an excellent match in every way."

"Perhaps she left her heart in the South. I've thought I could see a change in her ever since her visit there. Well, I don't believe her mother's in any hurry to have her marry and leave, for there never was a better daughter or sister. I've heard Mrs. Keith say more than once that she didn't know how she could ever do without Mildred."

"And she may well say so," joined in Mrs. Prior. "The other two are uncommon nice girls, but Mildred bears off the palm, to my thinking. I hear folks wondering now and then how it is that Mr. Lord has lived single all these years. I don't profess to know anything for certain about it, but I've strong suspicions that he's tried for Mildred Keith and couldn't get her, and he can't be content to take anybody else."

"She seems cut out for a minister's wife," remarked one of the others.

"Yes; she'd make a good one, I don't doubt," assented Mrs. Prior, "but I don't blame her for refusing him (if she has done it). It's a kind of a hard life, and he's too old for her and too absent-minded and odd."

The girls—Mildred and her mates—were talking over the arrangements for the approaching nuptials. The young men wanted a double wedding, and the girls were not averse to the idea. But the parents of each wanted to see their own daughter married beneath their own roof.

"My father says the ceremony ought to be performed in his house, since one of the contracting parties in each case is his child," said Claudina; "but Dr. Grange can't see the force of the argument."

"No," said Lu, "both he and mother say that it is always at the house of the bride's parents the ceremony should be performed."

"Can't you compromise by having it in the church?" asked Mildred.

"That is what we'll have to do, I presume," said Claudina, "if we are to have a double wedding. Oh, Mildred, if you and Wallace would only make up a match and let us have a triple one, I think it would be just splendid!"

"So do I," chimed in Lu. "Now what's to hinder?"

"A good deal," replied Mildred with a smile and a blush. "I doubt if it wouldn't make three or four people unhappy for life."

"What can you mean? I've been perfectly sure for years past that Wallace adored you," was Claudina's surprised exclamation.

Mildred's only reply was a quiet smile.

"And I daresay he must have popped the question before this," Claudina went on teasingly. "So, now do be good and obliging enough to fall in with my plan, for it's a capital one. Isn't in, Lu?"

"Oh, just lovely!" was the eager rejoinder. "Mildred, do! That's a dear!"

"Indeed, girls," Mildred said, her eyes dancing with merriment, "I do like to oblige, but in this instance it is beyond the bounds of possibility.

Whatever you may think, Wallace does not want me, nor I him."

"Well, then, all I have to say is that neither of you has good taste. And I'd set my heart on the match," Claudina said in pretended indignation.

Meanwhile, the younger girls were chatting merrily among themselves, flitting lightly from one theme to another—school affairs, parties, dress and beaux—teasing each other about the latter, as young girls will.

Zillah and Ada came in for their share. "Which was Wallace Ormsby courting?" they were asked.

"Probably both," Ada answered in a tone of irony. "He is a man of original ideas and doesn't always do things by rule."

"And he knows we can't live apart," added Zillah, blushing and smiling.

"Nonsense! He can't marry you both. Now which of you is it?"

"Suppose you ask him," returned Zillah, the color deepening still more on her cheek.

"I declare, I've a great mind to! I believe I'll do it tonight, if I get a chance," laughed her tormentor.

It was the custom for the ladies to come to the society as early in the afternoon as practicable and stay to a plain tea and until nine or ten o'clock in the evening, the gentlemen joining them for the last hour or two—an arrangement which served the double purpose of interesting the latter in the good work in a way to draw forth their contributions, and to provide escorts for the ladies on their homeward walk.

There was a full attendance that evening. Among

the early arrivals came Nicholas Ransquattle, bowing low, right and left, as he entered the room. "Good evening, ladies. I'm happy to see you all." Then, straightening himself and throwing back his head (now grown very bald) upon his shoulders in the old, awkward fashion, he sent his dull gray eyes searchingly about the room.

"He's looking for you," Zillah's next neighbor whispered in her ear. "I heard the other day that he had said downtown, talking with some of the fellows, that he was going to cut Wallace Ormsby out. And there, just see! He's making straight for this corner. You ought to feel proud of your conquest, Zil."

"Not till I'm sure I've made it, Sallie—no, not even then,' Zillah returned somewhat scornfully; "since I should be but one among the multitude of his adorable angels."

Sallie laughed and nodded assent as Nicholas drew up a chair and seated himself between them.

It was the common report that he had courted every girl of marriageable age in the town, offering heart and hand to each in succession as they moved into the place or grew into young maidenhood. No one had accepted him yet; he had never been attractive to the softer sex and did not become more so with advancing years. Behind his back the girls were unsparing in their ridicule of his awkward carriage, homely features, and unbounded vanity and self-conceit. They had dubbed him "Old Nick" and "The Bald Eagle."

"Permit your humble servant to be a thorn between two roses, ladies," he said with another low bow as he seated himself.

"Provided you are a useful one, Mr. Ransquattle," replied Sallie, giving him a needle to thread. "They are of use sometimes, I suppose."

"Yes, Miss Rush, to protect the roses, which I shall be most happy to do."

"Protect them from what?" asked Zillah dryly.

"From rude and careless hands that would fain pluck them from the parent stem, perchance only to cast them neglectfully aside and let them die." And Nicholas glanced significantly toward Ormsby, who had entered the room at that moment and was bidding "Good evening" to their hostess.

Wallace caught the glance, noted by whom Ransquattle was seated, and flushed angrily.

"Roses must die whether plucked or not," remarked Sallie, "and the fingers that pluck them save them from wasting their sweetness on the desert air."

"You'll never be left to so sad a fate, Miss Rush," was the gallant rejoinder.

"I don't know," she replied, laughing and shaking her head, "There may be some danger if the thorns are too close when the gatherer of roses comes."

Wallace had found a seat near Mildred, and she noticed that as he talked with her he stole many a furtive and ill-pleased glance in Zillah's direction.

Mildred was folding up her work.

"You are not going yet?" he said. "It lacks a full half-hour of the usual time for dispersing."

"I know, but Mrs. Smith is very sick, and I have promised to watch with her tonight."

"Milly, I'm going home," Ada said, coming up at

that instant. "Mother will be lonely, perhaps, and I can work just as well there as here."

"But I must go now, and we must not leave Zillah to go home alone."

"No, but Ru will be here directly—"

"Let me have the pleasure of escorting you both, and I'll come back for Zillah," said Wallace, speaking hastily in an undertone.

His offer was accepted, and the three slipped quietly away. Mrs. Smith's house was the nearer and not much out of the way in going to Mr. Keith's, so Mildred was seen to her destination first, then Wallace and Ada walked on to hers.

Wallace expected to leave her at the door and return shortly to ask the privilege of seeing Zillah safely home also. But Mr. Keith called him in, saying he had an important matter to consult him about, and in spite of the young man's ill-concealed impatience to be gone, kept him there for more than an hour.

In the meantime, Ransquattle made good use of his opportunity, managing things so that, to Zillah's extreme vexation, she could not reject his offered escort without great rudeness.

"Forewarned, forearmed," she said to herself, thinking of Sallie's gossip as they set out. 'Twill go hard with me, but I'll prevent his getting his opportunity tonight," was her thought as she rattled on in the liveliest strain without an instant's intermission, talking the most absurd nonsense just to prevent her companion from opening his lips.

They had reached her father's gate before he succeeded in doing so. She had no notion of asking him in.

"Good night, Mr. Ransquattle," she said merrily, letting go his arm and stepping hastily inside as he held the gate open for her. "I'm much obliged for your trouble."

"Excuse me, Miss Zillah, for detaining you a moment, but I have something very particular to tell you," he said, hardly waiting for the end of her sentence. "You are a very lovely and charming young lady."

"Oh, that's no news! I've heard it dozens of times," she interrupted, laughing and taking a backward step as if on the point of running away.

"No doubt. But never, I am sure, from so devoted an admirer as your humble servant. Miss Zillah, I lay my heart, hand, and fortune at your feet."

"Oh, don't, Mr. Ransquattle," she interrupted again, half recoiling as she spoke. "It's a dangerous place to lay articles so valuable, lest perchance they should be accidentally trodden on."

"Can you have misunderstood me?" he asked, as it would seem in some surprise at her obtuseness. "I meant to ask you to marry me. Will you? But don't answer now. Take time to consider, and I will call tomorrow to learn my fate from the sweetest lips in the world."

He was bowing an adieu, but now she detained him. Drawing herself up with dignity, and speaking in a calm, cold tone of firm determinations, she said, "No, do not call, Mr. Ransquattle. I need no time to consider the question you have asked and will give you your answer now. I can never bestow my heart upon you, and therefore never my hand. Good night, sir." Turning, she hastened with a quick, light step toward the house.

In the hall she met Wallace, who had just left her father in the sitting room busy over some law papers.

"Zillah!" he exclaimed. "What is it? What has happened?"

"Why do you ask? Why do you think anything has happened?" she returned, half averting her face.

"Because you look so flushed and indignant. If anybody has been insulting you—"

"Oh, Wallace, what nonsense!" she cried with a little nervous laugh.

"Well, I'm glad if it is not so," he said. "I hope no one would dare. I meant to go back to the society directly, hoping to have the pleasure of seeing you home, but I was unavoidably detained. It's early yet, though, and such a lovely moonlight evening. Won't you take a little stroll with me?"

"If you'll wait a moment till I tell mother we're going."

Mildred, finding she was not needed at Mrs. Smith's, had returned home and was just ready for bed. She had blown out her candle and was standing by the window gazing out and thinking how lovely everything looked in the moonlight when her door opened softly and the next instant Zillah's arms were about her neck, her face half hidden on her shoulder.

"How you tremble!" Mildred said, putting an arm around the slender waist. "Has anything gone wrong?"

"Oh, Milly, such a funny time I've had in the last hour or two!" she said, and the eyes that looked up into Mildred's face were fairly dancing with merriment. "I seem destined to play second fiddle to you, so far as the admiration of the other sex is concerned, having actually received proposals of marriage from two of your old beaux in this one evening."

"Indeed! Well, I hope you did not accept both," Mildred said laughingly.

"Not both, but one," she whispered with a low, joyous laugh, displaying a blush that was visible even in the moonlight. "Oh, Milly, I'm so happy! I don't care if I am taking what you refused. Wallace is far beyond my deserts, and I wouldn't exchange him for a king."

"Wallace! Oh, Zillah, how glad I am! I need no longer feel remorseful for having wrecked his happiness, and I shall rejoice to call him brother. He will be one to be proud of."

"Yes, I am obliged to you for rejecting him, and I daresay, so is he now," she added saucily, her eyes again dancing with fun.

"I don't doubt it. And now perhaps there'll be a triple wedding after all."

"What are you talking about?" returned Zillah in astonishment; "'tisn't time to be thinking of weddings yet."

"It would be too soon," Mildred said, going on to explain the occasion for her remark. The she added, "But you haven't told me whose was the other offer."

"Oh, can't you guess?" laughed Zillah; "don't you know that the Bald Eagle is still in quest of a mate?"

"Old Nick was it? Now then, you must just tell the whole story," Mildred said in a tone of amusement.

"'Twas quite a variation from his offer to you," Zillah answered mirthfully and went on to give a detailed and amusing account of the walk home and the short colloquy at the gate.

Bidding goodnight, she hastened to her own room, shared with Ada, and repeated the story to her, winding up with, "Your turn will come, you may depend upon that, so try to be prepared."

"Small need of preparation," was the cool rejoinder. "But you've had a walk with Wallace since. Won't you tell me what he said.

"I couldn't begin to remember it all, but—Ada, darling, can you spare me to him?"

The last words were spoken in a tremulous half-whisper, her arms about her sister's neck, her lips close to her ear.

"I knew 'twould come to that before long!" sighed Ada with a hug and a kiss while tears sprang to her eyes. "Oh, Zillah, dear, I believe my happiest days are over and gone!"

"No! No, no, darling! The very, very sweetest are yet to come! Love will be yours someday, as it is mine tonight, and

> *"'There's nothing half so sweet in life*
> *As love's young dream.'"*

CHAPTER XVII

But happy they! The happiest of their kind!
Whom gentler stars unite, and in one fate
Their hearts, their fortunes, and their beings blend.

Wallace Ormsby sought and obtained a second interview with Mr. Keith that evening, in which he asked his senior partner to take him into still closer relations and bestow upon him a priceless gift.

Mr. Keith was both surprised and moved. "I can't realize that she's really grown up," he said, "and—I don't know how to spare her even to you, Wallace."

"But you know, my dear sir, it isn't as if I wanted to carry her away."

"No, that's quite true. But her mother's right in her is fully equal to mine. Wait a moment till I call her in."

So the request and the arguments in its favor had to be repeated.

The mother's eyes filled, and for a moment she was silent. Then, holding out her hand to the young man, she said, "I have long had a motherly affection for you, Wallace, and there is no one else to whom I could so willingly entrust the happiness of my dear child—yet it is very hard to give her up."

"Don't think of it in that way, dear Mrs. Keith," he answerd in tones of the deepest respect, taking the

176

hand and lifting it gallantly to his lips. "Think of it rather as taking another member, another son, into the family. It would be joy to me to have the right to call you mother."

"And I should be very proud to own you as my son," she returned with her own sweet, motherly smile. "But Zillah herself must decide this question."

"Then I have nothing to fear, nothing more to ask," he said joyously.

In truth, no one had any objection to bring against the match, and all went smoothly and happily with the newly affianced pair.

The next day, Wallace came hurrying in with beaming countenance and eager air. "Ah! It was you I wanted," he said, finding his betrothed alone in the parlor, where she had betaken herself for her daily hour of practice on the piano. "Won't you put on a shawl and bonnet and come with me?"

"Where?" she asked with a merry twinkle in her eye.

"Just across the street to look at that house of Miller's. It's nearly finished, and he's willing to sell."

"But who wants to buy?" she asked in her pretty saucy way as she stepped into the hall and tied on a bonnet which she took from the hat rack there while Wallace threw a shawl about her shoulders.

"Perhaps we can better answer that question after we've been over it," he said with a smile.

So it proved. The snug, pretty, conveniently arranged cottage—so close to the old home, too—seemed just the thing for them. Father, mother, and all the family were presently brought over to look at and pronounce an opinion about it, and without a dissenting voice the purchase was decided upon.

"And now there's another and still more important matter to be settled," whispered Wallace in Zillah's ear.

"There's no hurry," she answered, blushing.

"There is to be a double or a triple wedding in our church in about a month from now," he went on lightly and in coaxing tones. "I want it to be the latter; so do four other people. But it all depends on you. Come, darling, why should we wait longer than that?"

"Ah, it fairly frightens me to think of such haste," she said, half averting her blushing face.

"I don't know why it should," he responded, his tone speaking disappointment and chagrin, "unless you fear to trust your happiness to my keeping."

"That's because men are so different from women. But to save a quarrel, we'll leave it to father's and mother's decision, shan't we?"

And she turned to him again with a smile so arch and sweet that he consented at once and sealed the promise with a kiss.

Father and mother said, "Wait at least until next spring. You are both young enough, and we cannot part so suddenly with our dear child."

"Hardly a parting—just to let her cross the street," Wallace answered with a sigh that was not altogether of resignation. Then he added a hint that he would be willing to leave her in her father's house until spring if only they would let him join her there.

But that proposal was smilingly rejected, and the wedding day was indefinitely postponed until "sometime in the spring."

Intimate friends were not kept in ignorance of the engagement, and the two expectant brides and bridegrooms were, until convinced of its uselessness, very urgent for the triple wedding.

The double took place at the appointed time and place, was quite a brilliant affair, and was followed by a round of festivities such as the quiet little town had never witnessed before. Evening entertainments were given by the Chetwoods, the Granges, the Keiths, and one or two others. Then life settled back into the ordinary grooves, and the rest of the fall and winter passed without any unusual excitement.

The Keiths were quietly, cheerfully busy, as at other times. Wallace came and went as before but was oftener left to Zillah's sole entertainment, yet he was treated more entirely than ever as one of the family.

Brighter days were dawning for our friends. Through all these years they had been very diligent in business and very faithful in paying tithes of all they possessed, and the truth of Scripture declarations and promises—"the hand of the diligent maketh rich," and "so shall thy barns be filled with plenty and thy presses burst out with new wine"—was being verified in their experience. This fall, Messrs. Keith & Ormsby found themselves successful in several very important cases, which brought them both fame and money. The town was now growing rapidly, business was looking up, and land, which they had bought for a trifle on first coming to the place, had already doubled and trebled in value.

Rupert, too, was succeeding well in his chosen vocation, and both he and his father urged Mildred to cease her toil as a music teacher, saying there was now not the slightest necessity for such exertion on her part.

The mother's views coincided with theirs, but Mildred begged to be permitted to go on in the old way, saying constant employment was good for her; she was used to it and liked it.

"And besides," she added playfully, "I enjoy the thought that I am laying a little something by against old age or a rainy day. I am not likely ever to marry, so will do well to be self-helpful. And why should I not have a business the same as if I were a man? I shall be happier, the more useful, and the more independent."

So they let her have her way. She was not keeping employment from those who needed it, for there were plenty of pupils for all the teachers in the place. Effie Prescott was now one of these—most faithful and successful, and full of joy and thankfulness that thus she was able to win her bread, for she had not strength to do so in any more laborious way, and her father was poor enough to feel it a relief to have Effie supporting herself.

"And I have you to thank for it," she had said again and again to Mildred. "It is one of your good works, and I shall never cease to be grateful to you for it."

"Indeed, Effie, you owe me nothing," Mildred would reply, "not even gratitude, for you have paid well for all I have done for you. You owe it all, under God, to your own industry, energy, and persever-ance in the use and improvement of the talents He has given you."

To the whole household at Mr. Keith's, the all-absorbing interest was the fitting up and furnishing of the snug cottage across the street and the preparation of Zillah's trousseau, in the expense or labor of which each one was determined to have a share.

All these matters were freely discussed in the family, even the little boys and girls being deemed worthy to be trusted not to speak of them to outsiders. Not that anyone felt that there was any special cause for concealment of their plans or doings, but they did not wish to have them canvassed and commented upon by the busybodies and gossips of the town, who, like those of other places, always knew so much more of their neighbors' affairs than did those neighbors themselves.

No one rejoiced more sincerely than Mildred in the evident happiness of the affianced pair; no one entered more heartily into their plans, was oftener consulted in regard to them, or was more generous with money and labor in carrying them out. Her sisterly pride in Zillah's beauty was without a touch of envy or jealousy, though she was fully aware of the fact that it far exceeded her own.

"What a lovely bride she will make!" Mildred often whispered to herself. "Wallace may feel consoled for my rejection of his suit."

She tried hard for perfect unselfishness and to entirely fill her mind and heart with the interests of the hour, especially as affecting these two. But thoughts of the love that now seemed lost to her, of the dreams of happiness which had been for years gradually fading till there was scarcely a vestige of them left, would at times intrude themselves, filling her with a sadness she could scarcely conceal from the watchful eyes of the tender mother who knew and so fully sympathized in the sorrows and anxieties of this firstborn and dearly loved child.

She knew that even yet there was a constant longing, a half-unconscious daily looking-for of news of the wanderer as the mail came in, followed each time by the renewed disappointment, and often her poor, weary heart grew sick indeed with hope deferred.

As spring opened, the day for the wedding drew near, and the preparations for it were almost completed. Mildred's sadness of heart increased until it cost her a constant and often heroic struggle to maintain her cheerfulness before others, while at times she could not refrain from shedding many tears in the privacy of her own room. One evening her mother, entering softly, found her weeping.

"My dear, dear child!" she whispered, taking her in her arms and caressing her tenderly, "My dear, brave, unselfish girl! You do not know how your mother loves you!"

"Precious mother!" responded the weeping girl, hastily wiping her tears and returning the caress. "What could I ever do without your dear love! I am ashamed of my depression, ashamed that I should yield to it in this way. Ah, I little deserve to be called brave!"

"It has been a long, hard trial, dear daughter," Mrs. Keith said, softly stroking Mildred's hair, "and you have borne it wonderfully well, as you could not in your own strength, I well know."

"No, never! The joy of the Lord has been my strength, else my heart would have broken long ago, for oh, this terrible suspense is so much worse than any certainty could be!"

"I know it, darling," her mother responded in moved tones. "Then would it not be your wisest course to endeavor to convince yourself that either utter indifference or death has ended this for you?"

"Mother, that is not in the power of my will. That Charlie could prove untrue I cannot believe, and something tells me that he still lives."

"Then, dearest, cheer up. Why this increased sadness of late?"

"I hardly know myself, mother dear. I am sure my whole heart rejoices in the happiness of my sister and Wallace, yet somehow the sight of it seems to deepen my own sorrow by contrast. I fear it is because I am selfish."

"I cannot think so," her mother said. "So do not harbor that thought, thus adding to your distress. Try to cast your care on the Lord, fully believing the inspired declaration that 'all things work together for good to them that love God, to them who are called according to His purpose.' He is never for a moment unmindful of one of His children; He has a plan for each one and suffers no real evil to befall them. 'Rest in the Lord, and wait patiently for Him.'"

"Ah, mother," Mildred said, smiling through her tears, "I am more and more convinced that all I need to make me perfectly happy is strong, unwavering faith in the wisdom and love of my heavenly Father. Then I should rejoice to do and suffer all His holy will, never doubting that what He sends is the very best for me."

There was an additional cause for Mildred's depression just at this time, one felt in greater or lesser degree by all the Keiths, in the thought that this was the beginning of the inevitable breaking up of the dear family circle, the forming by one of their number of new ties, which must in some measure supplant the old—the tender loves of parents and children, brothers, and sisters. Zillah was not going far away, and they did not fear to trust her to Wallace, but their home would no longer be hers, and another, in whose veins ran no drop of their blood, would henceforth be nearer and dearer to her than they.

Except for the parents, perhaps no other felt this quite so keenly as Ada—the nearest in age and hitherto the roommate and almost inseparable companion of the sister who was leaving them.

It was the morning of the wedding day. The ceremony was to take place in the evening, in the parlor of Mr. Keith's house, which the sisters were busily decorating for the occasion with spring flowers from the garden and the woods.

The supply was not sufficient, and the little boys were sent in search of some more. The mother and Celestia Ann—who still lived with them, going home occasionally for a few weeks, but always returning and taking up her duties there with renewed satisfaction—were deep in the mysteries of cake making and kindred arts, so when the door bell rang, Ada answered it.

Standing before the open door was a very pleasant-faced young man, whose dress and general appearance seemed to bespeak him a clergyman. He lifted his hat with a low bow, his face lighting up with a smile of recognition.

"Miss Mildred?" he said half inquiringly as he held out his hand in cordial greeting.

"No, sir," returned Ada, giving him her hand and a slightly puzzled look. "I am Ada Keith."

"Ah! One of the little ones when I knew you — not old enough to remember me, I fear. I am from Lansdale, your old Ohio home."

He handed her a card, on which she read at a glance, "Rev. Francis Osborne."

"Ah, I know now who you are! I have a slight remembrance of a big boy of that name who has had time enough to grow into a man," she said with an arch smile that he thought very bewitching. "Come in, Mr. Osborne, they will all be glad to see you."

He was warmly welcomed and hospitably entertained as an old-time friend, as one coming from the early home still held in tender remembrance, and as a messenger from Aunt Wealthy, who sent by him a handsome bridal gift: a beautiful gold brooch. That was quite unexpected, for the dear old lady had already given generously toward the house furnishing.

Zillah was greatly pleased. There was already upon a side table in the sitting room quite an array of handsome presents from her near relatives and friends — the Dinsmore cousins and others — and Aunt Wealthy's gift was now assigned a conspicuous place among them.

Mrs. Keith's wedding dress of rich white silk, her bridal veil and orange blossoms, had been carefully preserved, and finding that the dress exactly fitted her, Zillah had chosen to be married in it, in decided preference to having a new one.

It was, of course, made in a very old-fashioned style, but she insisted that she liked it all the better for that, and no one who saw her in it could deny that it was extremely becoming.

All the sisters were to be bridesmaids—in the order of their ages—and all were to wear white tarlatan. Rupert would be first groomsman; Robert Grange, a brother of Lu, second; Cyril and Don, third and fourth.

A large number of guests were invited, and a handsome entertainment was provided. Their pastor, Mr. Lord, had received due notice of the coming event and had promised to officiate.

Seeing him leaving the parsonage early in the afternoon, his mother called to him, asking him where he was going.

"For a walk and to make a pastoral call or two," he answered, pausing and turning toward her with an air of affectionate respect.

"Well, Joel, don't forget to come home early enough to dress for the wedding. I shall be ready in good time, and hope you will too."

"Oh, certainly, mother! I'm glad you reminded me, though, for I really had forgotten it."

"And will again, I'm very much afraid," she murmured between a smile and a sigh as she watched him proceed down the street.

He walked on and on in meditative mood, till nearing a farmhouse several miles from town, he was waked from his reverie by the voice of its owner bidding him good day and asking if he would go with him to the river for an afternoon's fishing. "I was just setting off for it," he said. "I've an extra pole and line here, and shall be glad of your company."

"Thank you, Mr. Vail, I will. It's a pastime I'm somewhat partial to," the minister answered.

"Will, Will!" the farmer called to his son, "bring me that other fishing tackle, and tell your mother we'll be back — Mr. Lord and I — for tea about sundown."

Seven was the hour set for the wedding ceremony. At half-past five Mrs. Lord's tea table was ready and waiting for the return of her son. But six o'clock came, and there was no sign of his approach.

"I'll go and dress. Perhaps he'll be here by that time," she said to herself, turning from the window from which she had been gazing with constantly increasing anxiety and impatience.

She dressed quickly, hoping every moment to hear his step and voice, but he came not. She ate her supper, watched the clock until the hands pointed to five minutes of seven, and then, filled with vexation and chagrin, donned bonnet and shawl and set off in haste for Mr. Keith's.

That gentleman met her at the gate. "Ah, my dear madam, I am glad to see you!" he said, shaking hands with her. "Please, walk in. But where is Mr. Lord? The guests are all assembled — now that you are here — and everything is in readiness for the ceremony."

"Indeed, Mr. Keith, I'm terribly mortified!" the old lady burst out, flushing like a girl. "It's just Joel's absent-mindedness. He meant to be here in season, I know, but he walked out some hours ago, and where he is now, or when he will remember to come back, I don't know. Please don't wait for him another minute, if you can get anybody to take his place."

"Fortunately, we can," said Mr. Keith, "so please, my dear madam, do not feel disturbed about that."

He led her into the house and called Rupert and Wallace from the bridal chamber, where the wedding party was assembled. Then Frank Osborne was summoned from the parlor, where, with the other guests, he sat waiting to witness the coming ceremony. There was a whispered consultation, then Wallace hastened to his bride again and whispered a word to her, to which she gave a pleased, blushing assent as she rose and suffered him to draw her hand within his arm.

In another minute or two, bridegroom and bride, with the whole train of attendants, had taken their places in presence of the assembled guests, and the ceremony began, Frank Osborne officiating.

He did not seem at all embarrassed or at a loss for words. His manner was solemn and tender, and when the ceremony was over, everyone said, "How beautiful it was!"

While the bride and groom were receiving the congratulations of relatives and friends, Mr. Lord, having leisurely finished his tea, sat on the farmhouse porch, quietly conversing with his host. But a sudden thought seemed to strike him, and he started up in evident perturbation.

"What is it?" asked Mr. Vail. "Anything gone wrong?"

"Rather," groaned the minister, glancing at the face of his watch, which he had just drawn from its fob. "I was to have married Wallace Ormsby and one of Mr. Keith's daughters about fifteen minutes ago."

"Better get back to town, then, as fast as you can," returned the farmer, laughing. "I'll harness up and take you."

"Alas, man, it's already too late!" sighed the minister.

"'Better late than never,' though, and they may be waiting for you still."

"Why, yes, that's possible, to be sure!"

"Where shall I take you?" Mr. Vail asked half an hour later as they drove into town.

"Drive right to Mr. Keith's, if you please."

"I thought maybe you'd want to fix up a bit, seeing it's a wedding you're going to."

"Oh, to be sure! Yes, certainly! I'm glad you reminded me. I'll go home and dress first."

"And while you're at that, I'll go round and tell 'em you're coming—just to keep 'em from getting quite out of heart, you know."

He went, and by the time Mr. Lord's preparations were complete, returned with the information, delivered in tones of amusement and with eyes twinkling with fun: "You've lost your job, sir; somebody else has tied the knot. But they've sent word for you to hurry along, and you'll be in time for refreshments. So cheer up, for that's the main thing, after all, ain't it."

"Really I—I'm ashamed to go now," stammered the minister, looking much mortified and embarrassed.

"Tut, tut, man! Better treat it as a good joke," returned the farmer merrily.

"I believe you're right," said Mr. Lord, and he proceeded to take the advice.

His apologies and excuses were received with good-humored raillery, mingled with laughing assurances that he need not disturb himself, since things had turned out all very well. It seemed a pleasant accident that had left the performing of the ceremony to an old and valued friend of the bride and her family.

Chapter XVIII

A lovely being, scarcely formed or moulded.
A rose with all its sweetest leaves yet folded.

— Byron

The next morning Mr. and Mrs. Ormsby started on their bridal trip—a visit to his relatives, to Aunt Wealthy and the old Ohio home.

Their departure left the house strangely empty and desolate, to the consciousness of mother and sisters especially, and Frank Osborne's advent seemed quite a boon. An old friend who could tell them much of others left behind in Ohio, a thorough gentleman, well educated, refined and polished in manner, and an earnest, devoted Christian, he proved a most agreeable companion.

All these years he had fancied himself in love with Mildred, and it was that, more than anything else, which had drawn him there. But the first sight of Ada had wholly changed the direction of his inclination.

He had thought Mildred charming in younger days and could not see that she had lost in attractiveness—the years seemed rather to have added to her loveliness. Her form was more finely developed and her countenance sweeter and more intellectual, while she had lost none of the freshness and bloom of youth. Yet he found a superior fascination about Ada, and being of an ardent temperament, open and frank in disposition, his manner toward her soon made this apparent to the older members of the family.

Mildred was perhaps the first to perceive it, and that without the slightest feeling of envy or jealousy. She would be glad if Frank proved to be one who could fill Ada's heart, and if an objection to the possibility that presented itself arose in any one's mind, it was merely on the score of unwillingness to part with another member of the newly broken family circle.

They had urged Frank to make a lengthened visit, and he had promised to remain for some days or a week or two.

He had been but recently licensed to preach and was yet without charge. The first Sunday after his arrival, he filled Mr. Lord's pulpit, by invitation, greatly to the delight and edification of his hearers. The next week, he preached for a vacant church a few miles distant from Pleasant Plains, and shortly after consented to take charge of it for the next six months.

A worldly-minded man seeking wealth and fame would have deemed it a most uninviting field of labor, but Frank Osborne was one of those who are willing to bear hardness as good soldiers of Jesus Christ and whose aspiration is to win souls rather than earthly riches or fame. Yet the thought of being near enough to his old friends to make frequent calls may have had its influence also.

The return of the bride and groom after an absence of six weeks was a joyful occasion. They were received in their own cottage home, which loving hands had set in perfect order and rendered beautiful and delightful with the bloom and perfume of flowers. When the tender, loving greetings had been exchanged, they made their tour of the house attended by every member of the family, each one anxious to witness and have a share in their pleasure.

The workers had anticipated, as the reward of their labors, great demonstrations of delight from Zillah, and they were not disappointed. She seemed to lack words to properly express her admiration of the effects produced or her appreciation of this evidence of their kindness and love.

Nor was Wallace far behind in bestowing a like measure of praise and thanks.

The welcoming feast had been prepared and was partaken of in the house of the parents. After that, Zillah began her housekeeping, enjoying it exceedingly, for she was no novice at the business, was deft-handed and quick in her motions, and had her mother and older sister near enough to be consulted at any time. Also, the utensils, furniture, and the snug cottage itself were all so new, so fresh and clean.

Then Wallace was pleased with everything she did, and the work of a family of two seemed scarce more than play to one used to the large household on the other side of the street.

There was a great deal of running back and forth, a constant interchange of good offices. During the hours that business kept Wallace at the office, Zillah and Ada were almost sure to be together in one home or the other.

It was not long before the former discovered that Frank Osborne was a frequent visitor at her father's and began to suspect what was the particular attraction that drew him there.

"I was not at all displeased at the time, as things turned out, that Mr. Lord went fishing on my wedding day and forgot to marry me, but now I begin to feel quite grateful to him," she said teasingly to Ada one day as they sat alone together with their sewing in her own pretty parlor.

"Why so?" Ada asked, blushing consciously in spite of herself.

"Because in later years it will seem very fitting that my brother-in-law did the tying of the knot between Wallace and me."

"That strikes me as very much like counting your chickens before they are hatched," returned Ada demurely. "If you are hinting at me, please understand that I've always meant to be the old-maid daughter, to stay at home and take care of the dear father and mother."

"Oh, yes, but folks often miss their vocation. However, I trust you will not, and I think you were cut out for a minister's wife. And, oh, Ada dear," she went on, dropping her work to put her arms about her sister, "I want you to know the bliss of wedded love. I never was so happy in my life as now. And I do believe Frank is almost as nice as Wallace, or at least nicer than anybody except Wallace," she corrected herself hastily and with a merry laugh. "So don't reject him; there's a dear."

"Not until he asks," Ada said a bit disdainfully. "My promises can go no further than that at present. I have an idea that he was formerly one of Mildred's admirers, so let him try for her. She is far better fitted than I for the duties and responsibilities of the position."

"Now don't be naughty and proud," Zillah said merrily. "You may as well take Mildred's leavings as I, and I can assure you they may be very nice indeed. What may have been in the past," she added more gravely, "I do not know, but very sure I am that now there is no fancy on either side."

"A letter for you, Ada!" cried Fan, running in through the open door.

Ada took it quietly and broke the seal.

"Now here's an offer worth having," she remarked with biting sarcasm as she turned the page and glanced at the signature, then held it so that Zillah could see what it was. "The bald eagle is still in search of a mate," she said.

"I told you so," was Zillah's laughing rejoinder.

"Lend me an envelope, will you?" Ada said, rising with the letter in her hand, a look of quiet, half-scornful determination in her face; "and he shall not be kept long waiting for his answer."

"What shall you say?" Zillah asked as she brought the envelope, pen, and ink.

"Nothing. Silence cannot be construed to mean consent in this instance. There, Fan, please return it to the office," she said as she sealed the envelope and handed it to the child, the letter inside, Nicholas Ransquattle's address on the outside.

The needles were plied in silence for a few moments, then Zillah said, with a little amused laugh, "You made short work with him."

"It seems to be the way of the family," returned Ada, joining in the laugh.

"Well, only treat Frank as differently as possible — that is, with the greatest favor — and I'll forgive you for this."

Frank was too wise to speak hastily, therefore the more likely to win at the last.

One day in the ensuing autumn Mrs. Keith received a letter from her cousin Horace Dinsmore, saying that he was traveling with his little daughter in the region of the Great Lakes and could not persuade himself to pass so near Pleasant Plains without paying her a visit. They might be expected in a day or two after the receipt of this communication.

This news was received with great delight by the entire family. Mildred's heart bounded at the thought of again clasping little Elsie in her arms, for through the years of separation the little fair one had been cherished in her very heart of hearts.

Every preparation was at once set on foot for entertaining the coming guests in the most hospitable manner.

There had been an occasional interchange of letters that had kept each of the two families informed of any event of unusual importance occurring in the other. Horace had written his cousin Marcia on his return from Europe two years and a half before this, again upon his recovery from serious illness a year later, and several times since. In one of is late letters he had spoken very feelingly of his child's recovery from an illness that had nearly cost her life, expressing his gratitude to God for her restoration to health, and that the trial had been blessed to himself in leading him to Christ.

Mrs. Keith had loved him from his early childhood with a sisterly affection, and now there was a new tie between them, for they were disciples of the same Master, servants of the same Lord. And it was in answer to long-continued, fervent supplication on her part that this priceless blessing had come to him. What wonder that her heart bounded at the thought of soon seeing him and little Elsie, whom she was ready to love almost as she loved her own offspring, because she was Horace's child and because of all that Mildred had said of her loveliness of character and person.

The letter telling of his conversion had brought a double delight to both Mildred and her mother, in the joy a Christian must ever feel in the salvation of a soul, the consecration of another heart and life to the service of Christ, and in the assurance that the darling Elsie was no longer left to an unsatisfied hunger for parental love. This the tone of his letter made very evident. His heart seemed overflowing with the tenderest fatherly affection, and indeed he said plainly that her death would have been worse to him than the loss of everything else he possessed.

But he did not go into particulars in regard to the nature or cause of her illness.

On the deck of a steamer rapidly plying her way down Lake Michigan sat a gentleman with a little girl on his knee. His arm encircled her waist, hers was about his neck. He was a very handsome man, apparently considerably under thirty years of age; hardly old enough, a stranger would judge, to be the father of the bewitchingly beautiful child he held. Yet there seemed a world of fatherly affection in the clasp of his arm and the tenderness of his gaze into the sweet face now resting on his shoulder, while the soft brown eyes looked dreamily over the water and now lifted to his with an expression of confiding filial love and reverence.

"Papa, I am having a delightful time," she said, softly stroking his face and beard with her small white hand.

"I am very glad, my darling, that you enjoy it so much, and I trust it is doing you good," he answered.

"Yes, papa, but I don't need it; I'm as well as can be now."

"Free from disease but not yet quite so strong as papa would like to see you," he said, with a smile and a tender caress.

"Shall we be long on this boat, papa?"

"Until some time tomorrow morning, when, if all goes well, we expect to land at Michigan City, where we will take the stage for Pleasant Plains, the home of our cousins, the Keiths. Do you remember your Cousin Mildred?"

"A very little, papa. I don't remember her looks, except that they were pleasant to me when she used to take me on her lap and hug and kiss me."

"Your grandpa wrote me that she was very kind to you. She's the only one of the family you've ever met."

"Please tell me about the rest, papa. Are Cousin Milly's father and mother my uncle and aunt?"

"You may say Uncle Stuart and Aunt Marcia to them, though they are really your cousins. Well, what is it?" seeing a doubtful, troubled look in the eyes lifted to his.

"Please, papa, don't be vexed with me," she murmured, dropping her eyes and blushing deeply, "but would it — be quite — quite true and right to call them so when they are not really?"

He drew her closer and softly kissing the glowing cheek, "I should prefer to have you call them aunt and uncle," he said, "and I cannot see anything wrong or untrue in doing so. But if it is a question of conscience with you, my darling, I shall not insist."

"Thank you, dear papa," she said, looking up gratefully and drawing a long sigh of relief; "but I want to do as you wish. Please tell me why you do not think it wrong."

"They may adopt you as their niece and you them as your uncle and aunt," he answered, smiling down at the grave, earnest little face.

"What a nice idea, papa!" she exclaimed with a low, musical laugh, her face growing bright and glad. "That makes it all right, I think. I knew about adopted children and adopted parents, but I didn't think of any other adopted relations."

"But do you not see that that must follow as a matter of course?"

A middle-aged woman had drawn near carrying a light shawl. "De air gettin' little bit cool, I tink," she remarked. "I'se 'fraid my chile cotch cold."

"Quite right, Aunt Chloe," he returned, taking the shawl from her and wrapping it carefully about the little girl.

But he had scarcely done so when a sudden storm of wind came sweeping down upon the lake from the northwest and drove them into the cabin.

There were other passengers, but the salon was not crowded and for a time proved a pleasant enough retreat. Supper was served presently and partaken of in tolerable comfort, though the lake was growing rough and the vessel rolling and pitching in a way that made it a little difficult to keep dishes on the table and eat and drink without accident. But, as they were not supposed to be in danger, the little mishaps merely gave occasion for mirth and pleasantry.

But before long, the storm increased in violence, the wind blowing a gale, accompanied by thunder, lightning, and torrents of rain. The faces of men and women grew pale and anxious, conversation had almost ceased, and scarcely a sound was heard but the war of the elements mingled with the heavy tread of the sailors and the hoarse commands of the captain and mate.

The little girl, seated on a sofa by her father's side, crept closer to him and whispered, "Papa, is there any danger?"

"I'm afraid there is, my darling," he said, putting his arm about her and drawing her closer still, "but we will trust in Him who holds the winds and the waters in the hollow of His hand. I do not need to remind my little Elsie that no real evil can befall us if we are His children."

"No, papa. And, oh, how sweet it is to know that!"

"It is your bedtime," he said, glancing at his watch.

"But you will not send me away from you tonight, dear papa?" she said, looking pleadingly into his face.

"No, my precious child! No, indeed! Not for all I am worth would I let you out of my sight in this storm, but I will go with you to your stateroom."

He half led, half carried her, for the vessel was now plunging so madly through the water, with such rolls and lurches, that it was no easy matter for a landsman to keep his feet.

They found Aunt Chloe in the stateroom waiting to prepare her nursling for her night's rest, but Mr. Dinsmore dismissed her, saying Elsie should not be undressed as there was no knowing what might occur before morning.

"Don't you undress, either, Aunt Chloe," he added as she kissed the child goodnight and turned to go. "Lie down in your berth and sleep if you can, but be ready to leave it the instant you are called. Give John the same direction from me, and tell him to keep near the door of my stateroom."

Left alone with his little girl, he knelt with her by his side, his arm supporting her while he commended both her and himself, as well as the others on the vessel and dear ones far away, to the protecting care of Him who neither slumbers nor sleeps. Lifting the child in his arms he held her to his heart for a moment, caressing her with exceeding tenderness.

"My darling, you shall lie in your father's arms tonight," he said as he laid her in the lower berth and stretched himself by her side.

"That will be so nice," she said, creeping close and laying her cheek to his. "It would make me glad of the storm, if I were quite, quite sure that the boat will get safe into port. But, oh, papa! If it shouldn't, I am so glad that you are not here without me."

"Why, my pet?"

"Because if you—if anything happens to you, I want to be with you and share it. Papa, papa, don't try to save me if you cannot be saved, too, for I couldn't bear to live without you!" she concluded with a low cry of mingled grief, terror, and entreaty as she clung about his neck, dropping tears on his face.

"God grant we may not be parted," he returned, holding her close. "We will cling together through whatever comes. But now, dearest, try to go to sleep, fearing nothing, for you are not only in the arms of your earthly father, but the Everlasting Arms are underneath and around both you and me. We have asked our heavenly Father to take care of us, and we know that He is the hearer and answerer of prayer."

"And I'm sure Miss Rose prays for us too, papa," she whispered. "She loves us so dearly, and I do believe God will spare us to her. But if He does not see best to do that, He will take us to Himself, and oh, dear, dear papa! I think it would be very sweet for you and me to go to heaven together!"

"Very sweet indeed, my precious one! Very bitter for either to be left here bereft of the other. But let us not anticipate evil. Still," he added after a moment's thought, "it is right and wise to be prepared for any event. So, dear one, should I be lost and you saved, tell Mr. Travilla I gave you to him, that I want him to adopt you as his own. I know he will deem it the greatest kindness I could possibly have done him and will be to you a father tender, loving, and true — a better one than I have been." His tones grew husky and tremulous.

"Papa, papa, don't!" she cried, bursting into sobs and tears, and clinging to him with an almost death-like grasp. "I can't bear it! I don't want to live without you! I won't! I will drown, too, if you do!"

"Hush, hush, darling! Do not talk so; that would not be right. We must never throw away our lives unless in trying to save others," he said, soothing her with tender caresses. "But there, I didn't mean to distress you so, and something seems to tell me we shall both be saved. Let me wipe away your tears. There, do not cry any more. Give papa another kiss, then lay your head down upon his chest and go to sleep."

She obeyed, and he clasped her close with one arm while the other hand was passed caressingly again and again over her hair and cheek. Presently, her quietude and regular breathing told him that she slept.

He lay very still so that her slumber might not be disturbed, but thought was busy in his brain — thought of the past, the present, the future; of the fair young girl away in a distant city, expecting soon to become his bride; of the beloved child sleeping on his chest; of the father who regarded him with such pride and affection as his firstborn, "his might and the beginning of his strength."

How would his death affect them in case he were lost tonight? Ah, Rose might console herself with another lover; his father had other sons; but Elsie? Ah, he was sure his place in her heart could never be filled. Travilla would be kind and tender, but — as she herself had once said — he was not her own father and could never be, even if he gave her to him. What a precious, loving child she was! How deep and strong was her filial affection! She seemed to have no memory of past severity on his part (ah, what would he not give to be able to blot it from his own remembrance, or rather that it had never been!), but seemed to dwell with delight upon every act, word, and look of love he had ever bestowed upon her. Ah, the bitterness of death, should it come, would be the parting from her, the leaving her behind to meet life's dangers and trials bereft of his protecting love and care.

But insensibly waking thought merged into dreams, and then his senses were wrapped in a profound slumber. At length he awoke to find that the storm had passed, the sun had arisen, and the vessel was nearing port.

CHAPTER XIX

The angels sang in heaven when she was born.

— LONGFELLOW

"Thank God, the danger is past!" came I a low-breathed exclamation from Mr. Dinsmore's lips. "Ah, my darling, did I wake you?" he queried as he perceived the soft brown eyes of his little daughter gazing lovingly into his.

"No, papa dear, I have been awake a good while but have not dared to move for fear of disturbing you," she said, lifting her head from his chest to put her arms about his neck, kissing him again and again.

"Did you sleep well, daughter?" he asked, fondly stroking her hair and returning her loving caresses.

"Yes, papa, I don't believe I moved once after we stopped talking last night. I hope you, too, have had a good sleep?"

"Yes, and I feel greatly refreshed. Our heavenly Father has been very good to us. Let us kneel down and thank Him for the light of this new day and for our spared lives."

They landed in safety, breakfasted at a hotel, and took a stage for Pleasant Plains, glad to find they had it to themselves—they and their two servants.

It was a lovely October day. The roads were good, the woods bright with autumn tints, the sun shone brightly after the rain, and the air was sweet, pure, and invigorating.

Elsie sat by her father's side, merry and happy as a bird—chatting, singing, laughing, and plying him with intelligent questions about everything she saw that was new and strange, and about the cousins whom they were going to visit. He answered her with a patient kindness that never wearied.

He had neglected her in her babyhood, and once—only a year ago—his tyrannical severity had brought her to the borders of the grave. He could not forget it; he felt that he could never fully atone to her for it by any amount of the tenderest love and care, but she would have all he could lavish upon her.

A joyous welcome awaited them on their arrival. Mrs. Keith embraced her cousin with sisterly love and his child with motherly affection, and Mildred wept for joy as she folded Elsie to her heart.

Indeed Elsie's beauty, her sweet, loving looks and smiles as she accepted and returned their greetings, won all hearts, while all present thought "Cousin Horace" far more agreeable and lovable than he had been on his former visits. There was less of pride and hauteur about him, more of gentleness and thought for the comfort and happiness of others.

Mildred and her mother were especially delighted with the ardent affection evidently subsisting between him and his little girl. Neither seemed willing to lose sight of the other for a single hour. She hovered about him, being almost always close at his side or on his knee, and he caressed her now and then, half unconsciously, as he talked.

Mrs. Keith remarked upon it to him as they sat alone together the day after his arrival, expressing her heartfelt joy in beholding it.

Elsie had just left the room with Annis, her father's eyes following her as she went with the wonted expression of parental pride and tenderness.

"Yes," he said with a sigh, "she is the very light of my eyes. Ah, Marcia, I shall never cease to regret not having followed your advice on my last visit, by taking immediate possession of my child! I have lost by that mistake eight years of the joy of fatherhood to the sweetest child ever a parent had. And yet it has, perhaps, been better for her, for I should have made her very worldly-minded instead of the sweet little Christian I found her."

"You have at all events escaped the loss I feared for you," Mrs. Keith said with a sympathizing smile.

"Of her filial love and obedience? Yes, she could not be more dutiful or affectionate than she is. And yet there was at one time a terrible struggle between us, but for which, I now see, that I alone was to blame. It was my severity, my determination to enforce obedience to commands that conflicted with the dictates of her enlightened conscience, which caused the almost mortal illness of which I wrote you. Yes, a year ago I had nearly been written childless. At one time I thought she was gone, and never, never can I forget the unutterable anguish of that hour." His voice had grown husky, his features worked with emotion, and tears filled his eyes.

Recovering himself, he went on to give her a some-what detailed account of the whole affair, as it is to be found in the *Elsie* books, she listening to the recital with intense, often tearful interest.

The little girls were in Mildred's room dressing dolls and chatting together, Mildred, busy with some sewing, overhearing most of their talk with both interest and amusement. Elsie was describing the Oaks and her home life there in reply to inquiries from Annis.

"What a lovely place it must be! And how delight-ful to have a pony of your own and ride it every day!" exclaimed the latter.

"Yes, it's very nice, but best of all, I think, is living in papa's house with him. You know we used to live at Roselands with Grandpa Dinsmore and the rest."

"But I should think you'd often feel lonesome in that big house with nobody but Cousin Horace and the servants. Don't you wish you had a mother like ours and brothers and sisters?"

A bright, eager, joyous look came into Elsie's face at that question. She opened her lips as if to speak, then closed them again. "Oh, wait a minute till I ask papa something!" she said, laying down the doll she had in her hands and running from the room.

Mr. Dinsmore was just finishing his sad story of her illness as the little girl came in. She heard his last, self-reproachful sentence, and coming softly to his side, she put her arm about his neck and her lips to his cheek. "Dear, dear papa, I love you so much!" she whispered. "Aunt Marcia," turning to Mrs. Keith, "I think I have the best, kindest father in the world. He was so, so good to me when I was sick, and he always is. To be sure, he punishes me when I'm naughty, but that's being good to me, isn't it?"

"I think so," Mrs. Keith answered with a smile, then excused herself and left the room for a moment.

"Papa," said Elsie, taking possession of his knee, "may I tell my cousins about Miss Rose?"

"I never forbade you to speak of her, did I?" he returned in a playful tone, smiling at her and stroking her hair with caressing hand.

"No, sir, but I would like to tell them that—that she is going to be my mamma soon, if I may—if you would like me to?"

"You may tell them; I do not object. But it was quite right to ask permission first," he answered. And with a joyful "Thank you, sir," she skipped away.

When Mrs. Keith rejoined him, he had another story for her ear—a brighter, cheerier one than the last, the same that Elsie was gleefully rehearsing to her cousins upstairs.

"Miss Rose was so nice, so good, so kind," she had been saying.

"Is she pretty too?" asked Annis.

"Yes, but not nearly so beautiful as my own mamma," Elsie said, drawing from the bosom of her dress a lovely miniature set in gold and precious gems.

Annis exclaimed at the extreme beauty of both the face and its setting while Mildred gazed upon the former with eyes full of a mournful tenderness.

"It's almost prettier than your gold watch," Annis said, "though I thought that was as beautiful as anything could be. Your rings, too."

"They were presents from papa and Mr. Travilla," said Elsie, glancing down at them, "and the watch was mamma's. Papa had it done up for me this summer and gave me the chain with it."

"Such a beauty as it is, too! Did you ever go to school, Elsie?"

"No, we had a governess at Roselands; now papa teaches me himself."

"Do you like that?"

"Yes, indeed! He explains everything so nicely and makes my lessons so interesting. He often tells me a nice story to illustrate and is never satisfied till I understand every word of my tasks."

"There!" cried Annis looking out of the window, "Zillah is motioning for me to come over. Will you come with me, Elsie?"

"If papa gives permission. I'll run and ask him."

"Why? Can't you go across the street without asking leave?" exclaimed Annis in surprise.

"No, I'm not allowed to go anywhere without leave."

"Now, that's odd! Your papa cherishes you so that I really supposed you could do exactly as you pleased."

"How Enna would laugh to hear you say that," returned Elsie, laughing herself. "She thinks papa is the strictest person she ever saw and says she wouldn't be ruled as I am for any amount of money."

"How do you mean? He seems so fond of you, and you of him, too."

"Yes, indeed, we're ever so fond of each other, but papa will always be obeyed the instant he speaks, and without any teasing, fretting, crying, or sour looks. And he is sure to punish the slightest act of disobedience, never taking forgetfulness of his orders as any excuse."

"Then he is strict," remarked Annis, shrugging her shoulders.

The two went downstairs together, Elsie asked and received the desired permission, and they hastened to inquire what Zillah wanted.

"I've been baking jumbles," she said. "I know Annis is fond of them hot from the oven, and I hope you are, too, Elsie. And here is a bag of candy Wallace bought last night. There, sit down and help yourselves."

Elsie looked a little wishfully at the offered dainties but politely declined them. Both Zillah and Annis urged her to partake, the latter adding, "I'm sure you can't help liking them, for nobody makes better jumbles than Zillah."

"They look very tempting," Elsie answered, "and I have no doubt are very nice, but I think they are richer than papa would approve. And besides, he does not allow me to eat between meals, unless it is some very simple thing that I will eat only if quite hungry."

"But the candy — you can eat some of that, can't you?"

"No, Cousin Zillah, I must never eat that unless papa gives it to me himself. Once in a long while he gives me a very little."

"Dear me! I begin to almost think Enna's right," Annis said laughingly.

"Oh, no, no!" cried Elsie, reddening and with tears starting to her eyes. "Papa is very, very kind to me; he forbids only what he thinks injurious to my health."

"Certainly," said Zillah, "and it shows that he is a good father. And you are a good daughter to be so ready to stand up for him and be so obedient."

She went out of the room, leaving the little girls alone for a short time.

"Annis, here is a note I want Wallace to have at once," she said, coming back. "Will you take it to the office for me?"

"Yes, if Elsie will go with me."

"I will go and ask papa if I may," Elsie said, tying on her hat. "Ah, there he is now coming out of the gate with Aunt Marcia."

She ran to him and made her request, Annis following close behind.

"Yes," he said. "Aunt Marcia and I are going to walk down the street, and you may run on before with Annis. I shall keep you in sight."

"Are you to wait for an answer, Annis?" asked her mother.

"No, ma'am."

"Then you and Elsie can join us as soon as you have handed Wallace the note. I am going to show Cousin Horace a part of the town he hasn't seen yet. Run on ahead, and we will meet you at the office door as you come out."

Eager for the walk with their parents, the little girls made haste to obey.

"There! My shoestring is untied," cried Annis, suddenly stopping short within a few yards of their destination. "Here, Elsie, won't you run in with the note while I'm tying it?"

Elsie obligingly complied.

The door stood open, and stepping through it she caught sight of a strangely uncouth figure: that of a man, coatless and hatless, wearing green goggles, a red flannel shirt with a white vest tied on over it, and sitting sidewise in Mr. Keith's office chair with his legs over the arm, dangling in air. A full set of false teeth twirling about in his fingers, he gave vent to the most dismal sighs and groans.

One sweeping glance showed the child that this was the only occupant of the room. Springing back in terror, she turned and fled, flying with swift feet to the shelter of her father's arms.

He was not far away, and in a moment she was clinging to him, pale and almost speechless with fright.

"My darling, what is it?" he asked, stooping to take her in his arms. "You are trembling like a leaf. What has alarmed you so?"

"Papa, papa," she gasped, "there's a crazy man in Uncle Stuart's office."

"Never mind; he shall not hurt you, daughter," Mr. Dinsmore answered in soothing tones.

Mrs. Keith and Annis were looking on and listening in surprise and bewilderment, then the former, seeing a tall form issuing from the office door, a coat over one arm and a hat in that hand, while the other seemed to be employed in settling his teeth, burst into a laugh, not loud but very mirthful. "Not a lunatic, dear, but our very odd and absent-minded minister," she said.

He was walking away in the direction to take him farther from them. They saw Wallace meet him and stop to shake hands and exchange a few sentences.

Then the two parted, Mr. Lord walking on and Wallace hurrying to meet them.

The thing was soon explained. Mr. Lord had come in overheated by a long walk. Finding no one in the office, he had pulled off his coat and settled himself to rest and grow cool while waiting for the return of Mr. Keith or Wallace.

But Elsie, with nerves still weak from her severe illness, could not recover immediately from the effects of her sudden fright. She still trembled and was very pale. So a carriage was sent for and a drive substituted for the intended walk, much to the delight of Annis, to whom it was an unusual treat.

CHAPTER XX

She was the pride
Of her familiar sphere—the daily joy
Of all who on her gracefulness might gaze,
And in the light and music of her way
Have a companion's portion.

— WALLACE

Wallace Ormsby was not behind his wife in admiration and liking for Frank Osborne. He enjoyed his sermons, too, and was desirous that Mr. Dinsmore should hear the young preacher and make his acquaintance; therefore, he had persuaded him and Mr. Lord to an exchange of pulpits on the morrow, which was Sunday, and invited Frank to be his and Zillah's guest. Wallace was hospitably inclined and not a little proud of his young wife's housekeeping.

The invitation was accepted and the visit extended a day or two by urgent request. Of course, the time was not all spent on the one side of the street, and Mr. Dinsmore, who was not lacking in observation, soon perceived how matters were tending between Ada and the young clergyman.

He spoke to his cousin about it, saying he was pleased with Mr. Osborne, finding him agreeable, well-informed, and an able sermonizer for his years, but surely his lack of means was an objection to the match — or would be if Ada were his daughter."

"Yes," she said, "But 'the blessing of the Lord, it maketh rich, and He addeth no sorrow with it.' If there is mutual love, we will raise no barrier to their union. But I should greatly prefer to keep my dear daughter with me for some years yet."

"Yes, I do not doubt that. I am glad indeed that it must be many years before I am called to part with mine to some other man. But, Marcia, how is it that Mildred is still single? So sweet and attractive as she is in every way, it must certainly be her own fault."

In reply, Mrs. Keith told him how it had been between Mildred and Charlie Landreth and how six long years had now passed with no word from or of the wanderer.

He was deeply touched. "It would be well if she could forget him and bestow her affection upon another," he remarked, "for surely if still living, he is unworthy of her. I knew and liked him as a boy, but it is long since I have seen or heard of him. He and his uncle suffered a disastrous failure in business, though I understand that no blame attached to either.

Then the uncle died, and Charlie disappeared from our neighborhood, where nothing has been heard of him since, so far as I have learned. But I will make inquiries upon my return and may possibly be able to trace him. However, rest assured that I will do nothing to compromise Mildred," he added, noticing a doubtful look on his cousin's face.

"Thank you," she said, her voice trembling slightly. "I can trust you, I know, Horace, and I cannot tell you how glad I should be to have my dear, patient child relieved of this torturing suspense."

This visit of their cousins was a grand holiday for all the younger Keiths, Fan and Annis more especially, since they were excused from lessons and had delightful daily walks and drives.

Every morning Elsie would take her Bible into her papa's room and spend a little while there with him before they were called to breakfast. He sent her to bed regularly at half past eight so that she was ready to rise early.

One evening when she came to bid him goodnight, he kissed her several times, saying, "I shall probably not see you in the morning, very likely not until tomorrow evening, as I am going hunting with your uncle, and we expect to start very early.

"Oh, I wish little girls could go too!" Elsie exclaimed, clinging to him. "But mayn't I get up in time to see you before you go, papa?"

"I don't think you will be awake, daughter. We start before sunrise."

"But if I am, papa, mayn't I run into your room and kiss you goodbye?"

"Yes, but try not to feel disappointment if you should miss the opportunity. And don't shed any tears over papa's absence," he added half in jest.

"No, sir. But it will be a long day without you," she said, putting her arm about his neck and her cheek to his.

"I think you will find the time will pass much more rapidly than you expect," he said cheerily; "but whether or no, you must try to be bright and pleasant for the sake of those around you. Don't indulge in selfishness, even in little things, darling."

"I will try not to, papa," she answered, giving and receiving a final hug and kiss.

No one was near enough at the moment to observe or overhear what passed between them, and no one knew anything about the few quiet tears Elsie shed as she went up the stairs to her Cousin Mildred's room, where she was to sleep that night. Ada, Fan, and Annis had all had their turn—because all wanted the sweet little cousin for a bedfellow—and now it was Mildred's. But she found her mammy waiting to prepare her for bed, and her little trouble was soon forgotten in sound, sweet sleep.

Mildred came up an hour later, and stepping softly to the bedside, stood for a minute or two gazing tenderly down upon the sweet little sleeping face. Its expression brought to her mind the lines—read she could not remember where:

I want to be marked for Thine own —
Thy seal on my forehead to wear.

"Dear little girl," she whispered, bending over the child, "you wear it if ever a mortal did! No wonder you are the very idol of your father's heart!"

Half an hour before sunrise, Mildred was again moving quietly about, careful not to disturb her little roommate while she went about dressing herself.

Going out, she left the door slightly ajar. Her cousin was just issuing from his, seemingly in full readiness for his expedition. They exchanged a pleasant, low-toned good morning.

"I did not know you were so early a riser," he said.

"I claimed the privilege of pouring out the coffee for you and father," she returned. Then, pointing to the door, she said, "Go in, if you like. I know you want to kiss your baby before you start. She's there asleep."

"Thank you."

He stole softly in and bent over the beloved sleeper for a moment, his eyes devouring the sweet, fair face. He stooped lower, and his moustache brushed the round, rosy cheek.

"Papa," she murmured in her sleep, but a second kiss upon her lips awoke her.

Instantly her arm was round his neck. "Oh, papa, I'm so glad you came! Please, may I get up and see you start?"

"No, lie still and take another nap, my pet. We'll be off before you could dress. There, goodbye, darling. Don't expose yourself to the sun in the heat of the day, or to the evening air. Though I expect to be back in time to see to that last."

"I hope so, indeed, papa, but you know I will obey you just the same if you are not here to see."

"I don't doubt it in the least," he said.

Then the door closed, and the little girl, accustomed to implicit obedience, turned over and went to sleep.

When Mildred came up a little before the breakfast hour, she found her dressed and reading her Bible.

"You love that book, Elsie dear?" she asked.

"Yes, indeed, cousin. And I do love to have my papa read it to me. This is the first morning he has missed doing so since—since I was so very sick." The voice sounded as if tears were not far off.

"How nice to have such a good, kind father," Mildred remarked in a cheery tone.

"Oh, it is so, cousin!" Elsie answered, her whole face lighting up. "I used to be continually longing for papa while he was away in Europe. I'd never seen him, you know, and have no mother or brother or sister. And now I just want to hold fast to him all the time—my dear, dear papa!"

"And you are missing him now? Well, dear, take comfort in the thought that he is probably enjoying himself and will soon return to his little dear daughter. I think he never forgets you—he asked what we could do with you today in his absence, and I told him my plan for the morning. He approved, and now shall I tell you about it?"

"Oh, yes, cousin! if you please," returned the child with a very interested look.

"Our sewing society meets this afternoon, and as we—mother, sisters, and I—have some work to finish before we go, we will have to be busy with our needles. One generally reads aloud while the others sew, and we would like to have you join us, taking your turn at both sewing and reading, if you choose."

"Very much, cousin, if—if the book is one that papa approves. He never allows me to read anything without being sure of that."

"Ah, that was why he said, 'Tell Elsie I say she may read or listen to anything her Aunt Marcia pronounces suitable for her.' We have some very nice books that may be new to you."

"Oh, then I think it will be ever so nice!"

"Well then," said Mildred, "we will take a short walk soon after breakfast, then spend the rest of the morning as I have proposed. Your papa says you can read aloud very nicely and use your needle well, too."

"I don't know whether you will think so, cousin," Elsie returned modestly, "but I am willing to try and shall do my very best."

They carried out their plan with only a short interruption from a caller. After dinner, Annis was left to entertain Elsie for a few hours while the others attended the meeting of the society.

It was an almost sultry afternoon, and Annis proposed taking the dolls to a grotto her brothers had made for her and Fan. It was near the spring that bubbled up at the foot of the high river bank and was reached by a flight of steps that led down from the garden behind the house.

The grotto was tastefully adorned with moss, pebbles, and shells, and had a comfortable rustic seat, artistically formed of twigs and the smaller branches of trees with the bark still on them.

It was a pleasant place to sit and dream on a summer afternoon, with the clear bright water of the river lapping the pebbly shore almost at your feet, the leafy branches of a grapevine overhead nearly concealing you from the view of anyone on the far bank or in a passing boat. A pleasant place, too, for children to play, and not at all a dangerous one. The little Keith girls went there whenever they chose.

Elsie and Annis were congenial spirits, enjoyed each other's society, and had spent an hour or more very agreeably together in this cool retreat when the sound of dipping oars near at hand drew their attention. Peering out from behind the leafy screen of the grapevine, they saw a canoe approaching, propelled by the strong young arms of Cyril and Don, now grown to be lads of sixteen and fourteen.

"Hello! We thought we'd find you here, girls," Cyril called to them. "Don't you want to take a row?"

"Oh, yes, yes, indeed!" cried Annis, jumping up and clapping her hands with delight. "Come, Elsie, there couldn't be anything nicer, I'm sure!"

Elsie rose as if the comply, her face full of eager delight also, but its expression changed suddenly.

"I'm afraid I ought not, Annis," she said. "Papa might not be willing, and I can't ask him, you know, because he is away."

The boys had now brought the canoe close up, and Cyril reached out his hand to help her in.

"Come, little coz," he said in his most persuasive tones. "I'm sure your father would not object; there isn't a particle of danger. I'm used to rowing on the river, as well as fishing and swimming in it—and it's not deep or swift, except in mid-current, and I promise to keep near the shore."

"But papa is very strict and particular," Elsie said, hanging back, though with a longing look in her lovely brown eyes.

"But he likes to have fun, surely?" put in Don.

"Indeed, he does, when it's quite safe and right," Elsie returned with warmth. "He loves me dearly."

"Then he wouldn't like you to miss this pleasure," said Cyril. "The canoe is a borrowed one, and it isn't every day I can get it."

"And if you don't go I can't," remarked Annis.

"Oh, yes, you can," Elsie said. "Don't stay for me. I'll go up to the house and amuse myself with a book till you come back."

"No, no, I couldn't think of leaving my company. It wouldn't be at all polite, and I couldn't enjoy it without you—yet I want to go ever so much. Oh, Elsie, do come!"

"I want to, I'm sure; both to oblige you, Annis, and for my own pleasure," Elsie answered. "Oh, I wish I were quite sure papa would be willing!"

"Take it for granted," said Cyril. "It's the best you can do under the circumstances, so he surely can't be much displeased."

Still Elsie hesitated.

"Ah," said Cyril, mischievously, "is Cousin Horace so very severe? Are you afraid he will whip you?"

"No," Elsie said, reddening. "Do you think so meanly of me as to suppose I obey my father only from fear of punishment?"

"No, and I beg your pardon. I know you're fond of him, too, and that you want to do right. But I have noticed that he is very polite and considerate of others, and don't you think he wishes you to be the same?"

"I know he does."

"Then surely he would tell you to go with us, because your refusal will spoil all our pleasure."

"Yes, Elsie, it was all for your sake we borrowed

the canoe," said Don, "and if you refuse to go it will be a great disappointment. We wouldn't urge you if it would be disobedience, but did your father ever say you mustn't row with us on the river?"

"No, Don, but perhaps that was only because he never thought of your asking me."

"Oh, Elsie, Elsie, do go!" entreated Annis. "I won't go without you, and I can't bear to lose the row."

"Didn't Cousin Horace leave you in mother's care?" asked Cyril.

"Yes."

"Well, then, what need of hesitation? Mother lets Annis go, and of course she would let you."

Elsie stood for a moment, silently weighing the question in her mind. Certainly her papa had great confidence in "Aunt Marcia's" opinion, for had he not said she might read whatever Aunt Marcia recommended? And he had left her in her care. Also, he did teach her to be considerate of the wishes of others; he had told her only last night not to be selfish in little things. Surely he would not have her spoil the afternoon's pleasure of these three cousins.

Ah, but he was never willing to have her exposed to unnecessary danger! But Cyril said there was really no danger, and—she did so want to go! It looked so pleasant on the water!

The scales were almost evenly balanced, and finally she allowed inclination to decide her, gave Cyril her hand, and was quickly seated in the canoe with the delighted Annis by her side.

Chapter XXI

Mutual love, the crown of all our bliss.

— Milton

The boys took up their oars again, pushed out a little from the shore, and rowed upstream for a short distance. Then, they turned and went down for a mile or more, keeping out of the main current all the time, according to promise.

Elsie felt a trifle timid at first and a little troubled that she had not done quite right in yielding to her cousins' persuasions. But gradually these disquieting thoughts and feelings passed away, and she gave herself up to thorough enjoyment of the present pastime.

They chatted, laughed, and sang; dipped their hands in the clear water; gazed through it at the pebbly bottom and the fish darting here and there; landed in several places to gather bright autumn leaves; then re-entered the canoe for another row.

The air was delightful, and most of the way they were pretty well shaded from the sun by the high bank and its trees and bushes.

The boys did not soon tire of their work, for their load was light, and going downstream required little use of their oars, and even rowing upstream was not very laborious. So the afternoon slipped away before they knew it.

"I believe the sun is getting low," Cyril said at length, "and we are a good mile from home. We must turn, Don. What time is it, Elsie?"

Taking out her pretty watch, she said in some dismay, "Half-past five, and the air begins to feel a little chilly. Don't you think so?"

"Yes, and it's suppertime. Come, Don, my lad, we must pull lustily."

"Yes, a long pull, a strong pull, and a pull both together," responded Don merrily as he bent to his oar.

"We ought to have brought shawls along for the girls," Cyril remarked with an anxious glance at his little cousin.

"I'm not cold," said Annis.

"But Elsie is. Here, little coz, let me put this round you," he said pulling off his coat. "Nobody will see you, and I wouldn't have you take a chill from this expedition for anything in the world."

"But you will be cold," Elsie said, shrinking back as he tried to put it about her shoulders.

"Not a bit. Rowing keeps a fellow warm as toast this time of year," he returned with a light laugh, and she made no further resistance.

Nearing the grotto, they saw Aunt Chloe standing at the water's edge with a shawl on her arm, looking out anxiously for her nursling.

"Oh, mammy! Has papa come?" Elsie called to her.

"No, darlin', I 'spect he'll be 'long dreckly. But what for my chile go off in de boat widout a shawl, when de ebenins gits so cool? Ise 'fraid he be mighty vexed 'bout it. And s'pose you'd got drowneded, honey, what den?"

"Come now, Aunt Chloe, it's all my fault, and if there's to be any scolding, I'm the one to take it," Cyril said good-humoredly as he helped Elsie ashore.

"Oh, mammy! Was it naughty of me to go? Do you think papa will be displeased with me?" the little girl asked in an anxious whisper while the nurse was busy wrapping the shawl about her, Cyril's coat having been returned to him with thanks.

"Maybe not. Dere, honey, don't you fret."

"Where was the harm in her going? But you won't tell of her, Aunt Chloe?" Annis said as they climbed the steps that led up the bank.

"No, chile, 'spect not; ain't no 'casion no how. Your papa neber in de house bery long fo' Miss Elsie tell him all she's been adoin'."

"Shall you tell him, Elsie?" Annis asked, turning to her cousin as they gained the top of the steps.

"Yes. I can't feel easy till papa knows all about it. I'm afraid I oughtn't to have gone."

There was a tone of distress in Elsie's voice, and, indeed, she began to be sorely troubled in prospect of her father's displeasure, for her mammy's words had caused her to see her conduct in going on the river in a new light, and she had now scarce hope that it would meet his approval. Besides, they were certainly late for supper, and he was particular in regard to promptness at meals.

They hurried into the house, expecting to find their elders seated about the table. But there was no one in the dining room, and though the table had been set, the meal was not spread. The ladies had returned but were waiting for the gentlemen, who had not yet come in.

Elsie was not sorry. She hastened upstairs to be made neat for tea, and came down again in a few minutes.

Still nothing was to be seen or heard of the huntsmen, and she began to grow uneasy. Perhaps some accident had happened to her dear papa. Maybe she was to be punished in that way for what she had begun to look upon as an act of disobedience or something very near it.

"Aunt Marcia," she said. Drawing near to Mrs. Keith, "what do you think makes them stay so long?"

"I don't know, dear, but nothing serious, I trust. They probably went farther than they had intended. But don't be anxious; I do not see any cause for alarm," was the cheerful, kindly answer.

Supper had been delayed a full hour already, and Mrs. Keith decided that it should wait no longer. "It is not worthwhile," she said, "for very likely our gentlemen have supped somewhere on the road."

Elsie was unusually silent and seemed to have lost her appetite. Her eyes turned every moment toward the door; her ear was strained to catch every sound from the street. Oh, what could be keeping her papa?

They left the table, and she stationed herself at a front window to wait and watch for his coming.

Mildred drew near, passed an arm about the child's waist, and with a gentle kiss asked, "Why are you so troubled and anxious, dear little girl? It is nothing strange that our fathers should be a little late in getting home tonight."

Then Elsie, laying her head on her cousin's shoulder, whispered in her sympathizing ear a tearful story of how the afternoon had been spent, and her fear that she had done wrong in going out in the canoe, and that perhaps she might be punished by something dreadful happening to her "dear, dear papa."

"I hardly think it was wrong, dear," Mildred said, "not a very serious fault, at any rate. And I cannot believe our Heavenly Father would visit you with such a punishment. He never treats us according to our deserts. He is 'a God ready to pardon, gracious and merciful, slow to anger, and of great kindness.'"

"Yes, I know; the Bible tells us that," Elsie returned, wiping away her tears. "How good He is to me and to all His creatures. It makes me ashamed and sorry for all the sin in my heart and life."

Mildred presently began talking of the old days at Viamede and Roselands, trying thus to help the little girl forget her anxiety. Elsie grew cheerful and apparently interested in her cousin's reminiscences of her babyhood; but still her eyes turned every now and then to the window, and her ears seemed attentive to every sound from without.

The clock struck eight, and with a sigh she drew out her watch and compared the two.

"Oh," she said, "why don't they come? I must go to bed in half an hour, and I do so want to see papa first."

"Do you think he wouldn't let you stay up to wait for him?" asked Mildred.

"No, cousin, he always insists on my going to bed

at the regular hour, unless he has given me permission to stay up longer."

The half-hour was almost gone—only five minutes left—when at last Elsie's ear caught the sound of a well-known step and voice.

She ran to the door. "Papa, papa! I'm so glad; so glad you've come! I was so afraid something had happened to you."

"Ah, I knew my little girl would be anxious," he said, bending down to give her a tender caress. "Well, there was nothing wrong, except that we went a little farther than we intended. And here we are safe and sound."

"And both tired and hungry, I daresay," said Mrs. Keith.

"The first but not the last," returned her husband. "We took supper an hour ago, at Ward's."

Mr. Dinsmore sat down and drew Elsie to his side. "Ah, is it so late?" he said, glancing at the clock. "Just your bedtime, daughter."

"Yes, papa, but—" and with her arm about his neck, her lips to his ear, she whispered the rest—"I want so much to tell you something. May I?"

"Yes. Go up now and let Aunt Chloe make you ready for bed, then put on your dressing gown and slippers and come to my room. I shall be there by that time, and we'll have our little talk. I should hardly like to go to bed without it myself."

Elsie obeyed, and he presently excused himself, on the plea of fatigue, for so early a retirement and went to his room, where she found him waiting for her as he had promised.

"Well, my pet, have you anything particular for papa's ear tonight?" he asked, lifting her to his knee.

"Yes, papa. But aren't you too tired to hold me?"

"No, it rests me to have my darling in my arms," he answered, caressing her in his tender fashion.

"Papa, I'm afraid I don't deserve it tonight," she murmured, hanging her head while a deep blush suffused her cheek.

I'm sorry, indeed, if that is so," he said gently, "but very glad that my little daughter never tries to conceal any wrongdoing of her own from me."

Then he waited for her to speak; he knew there was no need to question her.

"Papa," she said, so low that he barely caught the words, "I went out on the river in a canoe, with Annis, this afternoon. Cyril and Don rowed it."

"And my little girl went without her father's permission?" His tone was one of grieved surprise.

"But you were not here to give it, papa," she said, bursting into tears.

"A very good and sufficient reason why my daughter should have refused to go."

"But, papa, I did not know you would object, and I thought you would not want me to spoil the pleasure of my cousins, and they said I would if I refused to go."

"I think you certainly knew me well enough to be quite sure, if you had taken time to consider the question fully, that I would be far from willing to let you run into danger for the pleasure of others."

"But, papa, Aunt Marcia lets Annis go, and Cyril said there was no danger."

231

"Nonsense! Cyril is only a boy; not capable of judging. whether the current of the river is very swift and strong. I should not have trusted you upon it in a canoe with those boys for any consideration and am truly thankful that you escaped without accident. But I am not pleased with you."

"Papa, I am very sorry. Please don't be angry with me," she sobbed, hiding her face on his shoulder.

He was silent for a moment, then lifting her face, wiped away her tears with his handkerchief. Kissing her lips, he said, "I suppose the temptation was strong, and as it was not an act of positive disobedience to orders, I forgive you. But, my little daughter, you must never do anything of the kind again."

"No, dear papa, I will not," she said with a sigh of relief. "You are very kind not to punish me."

"Not kinder to you than to myself. It hurts me, I think, quite as much as it does you when I have to punish you," he said with another loving caress. "Now, darling, bid me goodnight and go to your bed."

CHAPTER XXII

All flesh is grass, and all its glory fades
Like the fair flower disheveł'd in the wind.

—COWPER'S *TASK*

Annis was in Mildred's room waiting to say goodnight to her cousin, rather uneasily, too, since she had gotten her into trouble by coaxing her into the canoe.

"Oh, Elsie!" she said as the latter came in, "was your papa displeased? Did he punish you? You look as if you had been crying."

"He said he was not pleased with me," Elsie answered, brushing away a tear; "that was punishment enough, I'm sure. But he forgave me the next minute and kissed me goodnight."

"Oh, I'm glad that was all!" Annis exclaimed, giving Elsie a hug. "I began to be almost afraid he had whipped you."

"No, indeed! He never did that, and I don't believe he ever will," Elsie said, a quick, vivid blush dyeing her fair face and neck.

The next day, the little girls were taking a walk on the riverbank, Aunt Chloe plodding along a little in the rear, so that she might watch over her nursling.

A boy coming from the opposite direction startled them by calling loudly, "Hello, Tim!" Where are you going?"

Two boys were just passing then, and the younger, who looked to be about ten years old, made answer in a surly tone and in words so profane that the little girls shuddered with horror.

"Well, I wouldn't want to go 'long with you, not to that place," remarked the first jeeringly. "But what's the use o' being so all-fired cross — swearin' at a feller just for askin' a civil question?"

"Come, Bill, just you let him alone," said Tim's companion. "He's worked up and mad, 'cause his mother told him not to go to the river, and that's where we're going this minute."

"Well, then, George, if he gits drowned, I guess he'll go where he said he was a-goin'," remarked Bill, walking on.

The little girls stood still, watching the other two as they hurried on down the bank, entered a canoe that lay on the water, made fast by a rope to a tree, loosed it, and pushed out into the stream.

They were not as careful as Cyril had been to keep near the shore, and presently the current was carrying them downstream very rapidly.

A few hundred yards below the spot where they had embarked, a wooden bridge had formerly spanned the river. It had been torn down shortly before this, but the posts were left standing in the water. Against one of these the canoe struck and instantly overturned, throwing the boys into the water where it was deepest and most dangerous.

The little girls and their attendant saw the mishap and ran screaming toward some men who were at work at no great distance. The instant the men comprehended what had occurred, they made all haste to the scene of the disaster and used every effort to rescue the lads.

They succeeded in bringing George out alive, but Tim had sunk to rise no more. They could not even find the body.

When this announcement was made, the two little girls, who had stood looking on in intense excitement and full of distress for the imperiled boys, burst into bitter weeping. They hurried home, crying as they went, to tell the sad story.

Mrs. Keith was in the sitting room, busy with some sewing, as usual, and Mr. Dinsmore was with her when the children came rushing in, crying as if their hearts would break.

"Why, my child, what is the matter?" Mr. Dinsmore asked in extreme surprise and alarm as Elsie threw herself into his arms and clung to him, sobbing convulsively.

"Oh, mother, mother! We've just seen a boy drowned!" cried Annis, burying her face in her mother's lap. "It was Tim Jones, and his mother had told him not to go to the river. And we heard him say such wicked words as he was going."

"And, oh, papa, he's dead!" sobbed Elsie. "And I can't even pray for him! Oh, papa, he has lost his soul!"

"We do not know that certainly, dear daughter," he said, trying to comfort her. "We may have a little hope, for possibly he may have cried to Jesus for pardon and salvation even after he was in the water."

"And Jesus is so kind, so ready to forgive and save us," she said, growing calmer. "But, oh, papa, it's such a little hope we can have that he did find the way and get a new heart in that one minute!"

"Yes, that is too sadly true," he sighed. "Yet the thought uppermost in my mind just now is, 'What if this had happened to my child yesterday?' Oh, my darling, how could I have borne such a loss? My heart aches for the parents of that boy."

"Dear papa, God was very good to us," she whispered, laying her cheek to his as he held her close to his heart. "Oh, I am glad he did not let me fall into the river and drown, though I was so naughty as to go without your leave."

"But I had not forbidden you," he said tenderly. "And I know my little girl loves Jesus and tries to serve Him, so I should have been spared the terrible pain of fearing that you were lost to me forever. Yet I cannot be thankful enough that I have you still, my precious, precious child!"

His tones were so low that Mrs. Keith could hardly have caught the words, even had she not been occupied, as she was, in soothing and comforting Annis.

CHAPTER XXIII

Oft what seems
A trifle, a mere nothing, by itself,
In some nice situation, turns the scale
Of fate, and rules the most important actions.

— THOMSON

Because of the near approach of his appointed wedding day, Mr. Dinsmore could not linger long in Pleasant Plains. All felt the parting keenly, for even in the few days they had spent together, a strong attachment had sprung up between Elsie and her cousins, and the renewal of former congenial relations had strengthened the tie of affection that had long existed between Mrs. Keith and her Cousin Horace.

Fan and Annis wept so bitterly as the stage whirled away out of sight that their mother and Mildred found it necessary to deny themselves the indulgence of their own grief in order to comfort the young children.

At the same time, Mr. Dinsmore was wiping the tears from Elsie's eyes and soothing her with tender caresses and the hope that she and Mildred and Annis would meet again before a great while.

"Who knows," he said in cheery tones, "but we may be able to persuade their father and mother to let them spend the winter at the Oaks next year!"

"Oh, papa, how nice that would be!" exclaimed the child, smiling through her tears. "Will you ask them?"

"Yes, if you will stop crying now. Perhaps if you keep on, I may be tempted to join you," he added jestingly, "and how ashamed we would both feel."

That made Elsie laugh. Then he interested her in plans for purchasing gifts for the cousins they had just left and for her "new mamma" when they reached New York, and soon she was her usual sunny self.

Fortunately, up to this time their little party had been the only occupants of the stage.

We have not space to speak further of their journey, which brought them finally to Philadelphia and Miss Rose Allison's home, where the wedding was to take place.

On arriving in that city, Mr. Dinsmore sent Elsie and her nurse to Mr. Allison's, while he, with his servant John, went to a hotel. He was to be married the next morning, and it was already late in the afternoon, so the separation would not be for long.

While taking his supper at the hotel table, Mr. Dinsmore became the unconscious object of close scrutiny by a gentleman seated nearly opposite—a rather fine-looking man, tall, well-proportioned, with good features, an open, intelligent countenance, benevolent expression, clear blue eyes, and light brown hair and beard.

"I can hardly be mistaken; it is no common face. But I will make certain," the stranger said to himself as he rose and left the room at the conclusion of his meal.

He went to the hotel register and found Mr. Dinsmore's name among those entered that day. He saw it with a thrill of pleasure, and yet—well, he could not know till he had tried to renew the acquaintance whether to do so would be agreeable to the friend of his boyhood.

Mr. Dinsmore retired to his own apartment on leaving the table and had scarcely done so when a servant handed him a card.

"Charles Landreth, M.D." was the inscription it bore. Mr. Dinsmore read it at a glance. His first emotion was surprise, the next a mixture of feelings.

"Show the gentleman up here; tell him I shall be happy to see him," he said to the waiter. Then, as the man closed the door and departed, he turned and paced the floor with slow, meditative steps.

"It may be a good Providence that brings us together so unexpectedly just at this time," he said to himself. "I should never have expected dishonorable conduct from my old chum Charlie Landreth, and I'll give him the benefit of the doubt as long as I can. Ah, God grant that I may be able to set this matter right for poor Mildred!"

Steps approached, the door opened, and the two stood face to face.

"Horace! You have not forgotten me?" The voice, the grasp of the hand, the beaming countenance, all spoke such sincere pleasure, such warmth of friendship, that Mr. Dinsmore's doubts vanished. That was not the face of a false, cold-hearted villain. He returned the greeting as cordially as it was given.

"Forgotten you, Charlie? No, indeed! And I'm particularly glad that you have made yourself known tonight, for tomorrow I shall be on my way south again."

"Ah, going back to the old neighborhood where we were boys together," Charlie said and heaved a sigh to the memory of the days of auld lang syne as he accepted a mute invitation to be seated. "Have you been long absent?" he asked.

"For several months. I am lately returned from Indiana, where I have been visiting my cousins the Keiths."

As he pronounced the name, Mr. Dinsmore looked keenly at his companion.

Landreth flushed hotly, and his look was both eager and pained as he responded, with a little hesitation in his speech. "Ah! And were they—all well?"

"Yes, thank you, and prospering. One of the girls—there are five in all—is married."

"Mildred?" asked his listener in a hoarse whisper and with half-averted face.

"No, she is still single, and it struck me as strange, for she is a most lovely and attractive girl in both person and character."

"A perfect woman, nobly planned,
To warn, to comfort, and command;
And yet a spirit still and bright,
With something of an angel light."

"I think I never saw one to whom Wordsworth's description was more truly applicable."

Landreth turned and grasped Mr. Dinsmore's hand, his face all aglow with hope and joy. "You have lifted me from the depths of despair!" he said.

"You have cared for her?"

"Loved her as never man loved woman before!"

Mr. Dinsmore smiled at that, thinking of Rose and and his early love, the mother of his child, but did not care to combat the assertion. "She is worthy of it," was all he said.

"I heard she was married, and it nearly killed me," Landreth went on. "But I could not blame her, for she had steadily refused to pledge herself to me."

"But where have you been all these years, and how is it that I find you here, Charlie? I should be glad to hear your story."

"I went first to the mines of South America," Landreth said. "Saw very hard times for the first two years, then met with a wonderful turn of fortune—coming quite unexpectedly upon a very large nugget of gold. I didn't stay long after that. I had written to Mildred a good many times but never received a line from her. And almost the first news I heard on returning to my native land was that of her marriage. As I have said, it nearly killed me, but, Dinsmore, my bitter sorrow and disappointment did for me what perhaps nothing else could. I sought and found Him, of whom Moses in the law and the prophets did write, Jesus of Nazareth, the sinner's Saviour and Friend."

"Thank God for that, Charlie!" Mr. Dinsmore returned with emotion, and again their hands met in a warm brotherly clasp.

"Having found Him," continued Landreth, "of course His service became my first object in life. I looked about for a sphere of usefulness and decided upon the medical profession, because I had discovered that I had a liking for it, the necessities of the men in my employ having led me to dip into it a little. So I came here to pursue my studies, received my diploma a year ago, have been practicing in the hospitals since, and am now looking about for the best place in which to begin my career as a private physician and surgeon."

"Plenty of room in the West," observed Mr. Dinsmore tersely and with a sparkle of fun in his eye.

Landreth sprang up. "And my darling is there, and you have given me hope that I may yet win her! Dinsmore, I shall make the necessary arrangements immediately and set off for Pleasant Plains at the earliest possible moment."

"Right, Charlie, and you have my best wishes for your success both with her and in your chosen profession. But I hope you will not leave Philadelphia before tomorrow noon. I want you at my wedding. Mildred and the rest will be glad to hear an account of it from an eyewitness."

"Your wedding?"

"Yes, it is to take place at nine tomorrow morning. And I want the pleasure of introducing my intended cousin to my bride, to say nothing of showing you whose charms of person and character are not eclipsed by even those of sweet and lovely Mildred Keith."

"She must be worth seeing, if that be the case," Landreth answered with a smile. "And I am keeping you from her now, I daresay, for which she certainly will not thank me."

"She is too kindhearted not to be more than content for Mildred's and your sake."

"Mildred's do you say?" Landreth's face was one glow of delight.

"Yes, Charlie, for Mildred's. Since you have so frankly told me how it is with you, I shall not conceal from you that it is for your sake the sweet girl has remained single in spite of several good offers. I learned it from my Cousin Marcia, her mother. And while I think of it," he added laughingly, "let me assure you that Marcia will make—does make—a model mother-in-law."

"I should be glad indeed to try her in that capacity," returned Landreth lightly. "I think it will hardly be possible for me to leave before tomorrow noon, so I accept your invitation with thanks, Dinsmore. I have a curiosity to see your bride and a very strong desire to renew my acquaintance with your little daughter, whom I used to see quite frequently in the first two years of her stay at Roselands. I have always thought her the sweetest little creature I ever beheld. She is with you, of course?"

"In the city? Yes, you will see her tomorrow," Mr. Dinsmore answered, looking highly gratified by the glowing praise the other had bestowed upon his darling child.

After a little more chat, principally of mutual friends and the changes that had taken place in their old neighborhood since Landreth left it, they separated with another cordial handshake, both extremely glad of the casual meetin, and expecting to meet again on the morrow.

CHAPTER XXIV

Within her heart was the image,
Cloth'd in the beauty of love, as last she beheld him,
Only more beautiful made
by his deathlike silence and absence.

—LONGFELLOW

It was evening, and Mildred was alone in the parlor, all the rest of the family having gone to a concert. They had urged her to go, too, but she had declined, saying she greatly preferred a quiet evening at home. Truth to tell, she was oppressed with sadness and wanted to be alone so that she might indulge it for a while without restraint.

All day she had maintained a cheerfulness in the presence of others that she did not feel, for there had been scarcely a moment when her lost love was absent from her thoughts. Why was it that her heart went out toward him tonight with such yearning tenderness—such unutterable longing to look into his eyes, to hear the sound of his voice, to feel the touch of his hand?

She tried in vain to read, but the image of the lost one constantly obtruded itself between her mental vision and the printed page.

She rose and paced the floor, not weeping but pressing her hand to her heart with heavy sighing.

The curtains were not closely drawn, or the shutters closed; a lamp burned brightly on the center table, and the room was full of warmth and cheer.

She did not hear the opening of the gate or a quick, manly step that came up the gravel walk and onto the porch. She did not see the stranger pause before the bright window and gaze in, half unconsciously, as if spellbound by the sight of her graceful figure and fair though sad face. She turned to the open piano, struck a few chords, then seated herself and sang in clear, sweet tones but with touching pathos:

> *"When true hearts lie withered*
> *And fond ones are flown,*
> *Oh! who would inhabit*
> *This bleak world alone?"*

Then, with a sudden change of feeling, she touched the chords anew and burst into a song of praise, her voice swelling out full and high like the glad song of a bird:

> *"Oh, the height of Jesus' love!*
> *Higher than the heavens above,*
> *Deeper than the depths of sea,*
> *Lasting as eternity;*
> *Love that found me — wondrous thought!*
> *Found me when I sought Him not."*

"A gentleman to see you, Miss Mildred," said the voice of Celestia Ann at the parlor door.

Mildred rose and turned to greet him in some surprise, for she had not heard the ringing of the doorbell or the sound of the girl's footsteps as she passed through the hall to answer it.

The latter retreated as she ushered the stranger in but lingered a moment, peering curiously through the crack behind the door. She saw him step forward with outstretched hand, Mildred moving toward him with an earnest, inquiring look up into his face, then an ashy paleness suddenly overspread hers. She staggered and would have fallen, but he caught her in his arms, saying in low, tremulous tones as he held her close to his heart, "Mildred, darling, it is I! Oh, tell me, dear one, that you have not forgotten me!"

"I know'd it! I know'd there was somebody somewheres she cared for! And I'm mighty glad he's come at last, for her sake," chuckled Celestia Ann, nodding and smiling to herself as she retreated to her kitchen. "Though I'll be dreadful sorry, too, if he carries her off to some fer-away place."

To those two in the parlor, the next hour was probably the most blissful they had ever known. Dr. Landreth's story was briefly told, to be dwelt upon more in detail in future talks, and then—but we will not intrude upon their privacy.

Mr. and Mrs. Keith, returning from the concert, found their daughter seated by the side of one who was an entire stranger to them. Yet there was small need of introduction, for by the look of restful happiness in her face they knew instantly who he was and that all was right between them. From the first, all were favorably impressed by Landreth's open, intelligent countenance, polished manners, manly yet modest mien, and a few days of intimate association made him almost as great a favorite among the family as Wallace Ormsby—and the latter was not far behind the others in his liking of the newcomer.

Mildred was very happy, and all her dear ones rejoiced with her, especially when it became known among them that it was not Dr. Landreth's intention or wish to carry her away from them.

"No," he said, "I know too well how sad a thing it is to be fatherless, motherless, and without any other near relative to desire to separate the dear girl from hers. What I want is the privilege of sharing them with her."

"Which we will all be glad to have you do," returned Mrs. Keith, to whom the remark was addressed, tears of sympathy for his past forlorn condition glistening in her eyes. "We will rejoice to make you one of us, not for Mildred's sake alone but for your own also."

"Accept my heartiest thanks, my dear madam," the young man said with emotion. You may perhaps have some idea what it will be to me to have a mother when I tell you that mine died before my earliest recollection."

Not even to his betrothed had Charlie disclosed the fact that he was again a man of wealth. He merely assured Mr. Keith that he felt himself able to support a wife comfortably, having a good profession and means enough to live upon until he should become well established in it.

Pleasant Plains was now growing so rapidly, the surrounding country filling up so fast, that hardly a better location for a young physician could be desired, and he decided to settle in the town at once.

And now what was to hinder an immediate marriage? This was the question he urged upon Mildred and her parents but without obtaining a prompt and decided answer. The parents had given full consent to the match yet seemed very loath to resign their daughter.

Cyril sided with Landreth, because, as he said, he wanted to be present at the wedding. Since he was to leave for college in a few days, and felt certain they would not wait till he came back, his only chance was to have it take place before he went, so he coaxed and persuaded, overruled all objections, and finally gained his point.

"It won't be parting with her," he said to his father and mother. "They'll board at home at least till spring. I asked the doctor, and he's delighted with the idea." To Mildred he said: "What's the use waiting to make up a lot of finery? You can do that afterwards. You have two new dresses just made up for fall anyway, and mother's wedding dress that Zillah was married in fits you just as well and makes you look lovely. We can't get up as big a wedding as Zil's all in a hurry, to be sure, but I don't believe you care for that."

"No," she said, "I should much prefer having only relatives and a few very near friends."

"It would save expense to father and a great deal of fuss and trouble to mother," was the next and most effectual consideration he urged. "Then, too," he added a little mischievously, "Mr. Lord's away just now, and that will give you a chance to have the knot tied by your future brother-in-law, the same as Zillah did."

This last was a stronger inducement than he knew or suspected. She had an earnest desire to have the ceremony performed by her old friend Frank Osborne and was a little apprehensive of some blunder on the part of absent-minded Mr. Lord, should he officiate.

"Frank's to preach for us next Sunday," Cyril went on. "He'll stay over Monday if we ask him, and if you'll let me arrange matters, I'll appoint Monday evening for the wedding."

"How very kind in you," she returned laughingly.

"Come now, Milly, say yes," he continued, not deigning to notice the interruption. "I'm to leave on Wednesday, you know."

"Monday, Cyril! Why, that's wash day, and Celestia Ann won't—"

"I'll settle that," he interrupted, making a hasty exit from the room.

After a brief absence, he returned in great glee. "I thought I could manage it," he said, "and I have. She's delighted with the idea of a wedding that shall take everybody in town by surprise. She won't give up the washing but says she'll be up early enough to have it out by nine o'clock, and then she'll 'turn in and bake cake.' She'll bake some tomorrow, too, so there 'won't be no trouble 'bout the 'freshments, not a mite.' Now, Milly, haven't I taken the last stone out of the way?"

"Yes, you dear old fellow," she said with a look of sisterly love and pride into his bright, eager young face. "And it shall be as you wish. Mother and I have been talking over your plan and think it practicable. Also, that it would be too bad to disappoint you, to say nothing of someone else even more nearly concerned," she added with a charming blush and smile.

"That's a good girl! I knew you would! I'll run and tell the doctor." And he was off before Mildred could stop him.

Of course, Dr. Landreth was delighted. No one else raised any objection, and hasty preparations were at once set in motion.

Mildred thought she ought to be the busiest of them all, but mother and sisters would not hear of it. "You have been working for everybody else for years," they said, "and now it is your turn to rest and have a good time. So just devote yourself to the entertainment of the doctor, or to be entertained by him." Finding them determined to dispense with her assistance, Mildred submitted with good grace, the more so as Charlie managed to occupy her time and attention almost constantly.

He had arrived on Monday, and it was on Friday that her consent to Cyril's plan was given.

Mr. Dinsmore's visit had created quite a sensation in the town. It was reported that he had come for Mildred, but the advent of this stranger who, though lodging at the principal hotel, spent his days at Mr. Keith's, modified the rumors, and people were on the lookout to learn which, if either, was the favored suitor.

The wedding passed off very nicely, just at the time and in the way that Cyril had planned, and the next morning the gossips of the town were electrified by the news.

The bride had a great surprise that day in her turn. It came in the shape of a mysterious box directed to her, which on opening was found to contain a beautiful bridal bonnet, three dress patterns of rich silk — a delicate rose color, a silver gray, and a rich dark brown — gloves, lace ribbons, and flowers.

The whole family had gathered round to watch the opening and unpacking of the box, and each article was examined in turn with many exclamations of admiration and delight. At the very bottom they came upon a note.

Dear Milly:

A little bird has whispered to me that you are soon to be a bride, and Elsie and I are very glad for the excuse to send a few trifling gifts, which we hope you will do us the kindness to accept as tokens of the sincere affection we both feel for you.

Cousin Horace

There had been no time for parents and friends to prepare bridal gifts, and excepting a beautiful set of pearls Dr. Landreth had purchased for her before leaving Philadelphia, these were the first Mildred had received.

"How very kind and thoughtful!" she said, her eyes glistening with mingled emotions, "but how did they manage it? What time was there for shopping after Cousin Horace saw you, Charlie?"

"I should say by no means enough for the purchase of all these," Dr. Landreth answered, evidently as much puzzled as herself.

A letter from Adelaide Dinsmore, which arrived in the next mail, explained it. She had been present at Horace's wedding, acting as a bridesmaid, and had remained behind when he left with wife and daughter for their home in the South. She had executed these commissions for him and Elsie, adding some gifts from herself and parents. She wrote in a cordial, affectionate way and begged for a speedy reply telling all about the marriage, because she "could get nothing out of Horace except that there was to be one."

"Mildred, you must come out in bridal attire next Sunday," Zillah said with energy. "You're to wear the new bonnet and that gray silk. We'll have it made in time."

It was made in time, and very lovely Mildred looked in it. She was the focal point of all eyes, yet another bride shared the attention of the curious.

Years ago, Gotobed Lightcap had gone to a distant city to pursue his studies. Today, a licensed preacher of the Gospel, he filled Mr. Lord's pulpit and gave the congregation an earnest, able, well-written discourse.

After the service, he brought his wife—a pretty, ladylike little person—and with a proud and happy look introduced her to Mildred.

The two ladies shook hands cordially, Mildred furtively examining the other with curiosity, Gotobed regarding Dr. Landreth in like manner. Then Mildred introduced them, and they exchanged congratulations and good wishes.

The Rev. Mr. Lightcap was in many ways a vast improvement upon the young blacksmith of Mildred's early acquaintance, especially as regarded education, intelligence, and refinement of speech and manner.

Dr. Landreth was greatly interested in him and his story as told by Mildred on the homeward walk. And she was very happy in the assurance that she had not, even innocently, wrecked his happiness, yet she was happier still in the love that now made life's pathway look so bright before her.

THE END

The Original Elsie Classics

Elsie Dinsmore
Elsie's Holidays at Roselands
Elsie's Girlhood
Elsie's Womanhood
Elsie's Motherhood
Elsie's Children
Elsie's Widowhood
Grandmother Elsie
Elsie's New Relations
Elsie at Nantucket
The Two Elsies
Elsie's Kith and Kin
Elsie's Friends at Woodburn
Christmas with Grandma Elsie
Elsie and the Raymonds
Elsie Yachting with the Raymonds
Elsie's Vacation
Elsie at Viamede
Elsie at Ion
Elsie at the World's Fair
Elsie's Journey on Inland Waters
Elsie at Home
Elsie on the Hudson
Elsie in the South
Elsie's Young Folks
Elsie's Winter Trip
Elsie and Her Loved Ones
Elsie and Her Namesakes

6/19